HOME

HOME

TONI MORRISON

ISIS

LARGE PRINT

Oxford

First published in Great Britain 2012
by
Chatto & Windus,
A company within The Random House Group Limited

Published in Large Print 2013 by ISIS Publishing Ltd.,
7 Centremead, Osney Mead, Oxford OX2 0ES
by arrangement with
The Random House Group Limited

CIP data is available for this title from the British Library

ISBN 978–0–7531–9170–5 (hb)
ISBN 978–0–7531–9171–2 (pb)

Printed and bound in Great Britain by
T. J. International Ltd., Padstow, Cornwall

Slade

Whose house is this?
Whose night keeps out the light
In here?
Say, who owns this house?
It's not mine.
I dreamed another, sweeter, brighter
With a view of lakes crossed in painted boats;
Of fields wide as arms open for me.
This house is strange.
Its shadows lie.
Say, tell me, why does its lock fit my key?

CHAPTER
ONE

They rose up like men. We saw them. Like men they stood.

We shouldn't have been anywhere near that place. Like most farmland outside Lotus, Georgia, this one here had plenty of scary warning signs. The threats hung from wire mesh fences with wooden stakes every fifty or so feet. But when we saw a crawl space that some animal had dug — a coyote maybe, or a coon dog — we couldn't resist. Just kids we were. The grass was shoulder high for her and waist high for me so, looking out for snakes, we crawled through it on our bellies. The reward was worth the harm grass juice and clouds of gnats did to our eyes, because there right in front of us, about fifty yards off, they stood like men. Their raised hooves crashing and striking, their manes tossing back from wild white eyes. They bit each other like dogs but when they stood, reared up on their hind legs, their forelegs around the withers of the other, we held our breath in wonder. One was rust-colored, the other deep black, both sunny with sweat. The neighs were not as frightening as the silence following a kick of hind legs into the lifted lips of the opponent. Nearby, colts and mares, indifferent, nibbled grass or looked away. Then it stopped. The rust-colored one dropped his head and pawed the ground while the winner loped off in an arc, nudging the mares before him.

As we elbowed back through the grass looking for the dug-out place, avoiding the line of parked trucks beyond, we lost our way. Although it took forever to re-sight the fence, neither of us panicked until we heard voices, urgent but low. I grabbed her arm and put a finger to my lips. Never lifting our heads, just peeping through the grass, we saw them pull a body from a wheelbarrow and throw it into a hole already waiting. One foot stuck up over the edge and quivered, as though it could get out, as though with a little effort it could break through the dirt being shoveled in. We could not see the faces of the men doing the burying, only their trousers; but we saw the edge of a spade drive the jerking foot down to join the rest of itself. When she saw that black foot with its creamy pink and mud-streaked sole being whacked into the grave, her whole body began to shake. I hugged her shoulders tight and tried to pull her trembling into my own bones because, as a brother four years older, I thought I could handle it. The men were long gone and the moon was a cantaloupe by the time we felt safe enough to disturb even one blade of grass and move on our stomachs, searching for the scooped-out part under the fence. When we got home we expected to be whipped or at least scolded for staying out so late, but the grown-ups did not notice us. Some disturbance had their attention.

Since you're set on telling my story, whatever you think and whatever you write down, know this: I really forgot about the burial. I only remembered the horses. They were so beautiful. So brutal. And they stood like men.

CHAPTER
TWO

Breathing. How to do it so no one would know he was awake. Fake a deep rhythmic snore, drop the bottom lip. Most important, the eyelids should not move and there must be a regular heartbeat and limp hands. At 2:00a.m. when they checked to determine if he needed another immobilizing shot they would see the patient on the second floor in Room 17, sunk in a morphine sleep. If convinced, they might skip the shot and loosen his cuffs, so his hands could enjoy some blood. The trick of imitating semi-coma, like playing dead facedown in a muddy battlefield, was to concentrate on a single neutral object. Something that would smother any random hint of life. Ice, he thought, a cube of it, an icicle, an ice-crusted pond, or a frosted landscape. No. Too much emotion attached to frozen hills. Fire, then? Never. Too active. He would need something that stirred no feelings, encouraged no memory — sweet or shameful. Just searching for such an item was agitating. Everything reminded him of something loaded with pain. Visualizing a blank sheet of paper drove his mind to the letter he had gotten — the one that had closed his throat: "Come fast. She be dead if you tarry." Finally, he settled on the chair in the corner of the room as his neutral object. Wood. Oak. Lacquered or stained. How many slats in its back? Was the seat flat or curved for a bottom? Hand-crafted or machine-made? If hand-crafted, who was the carpenter and where did he get his lumber? Hopeless. The chair was provoking questions, not blank indifference. What about the ocean on a cloudy day seen from the deck of a troopship — no horizon or hope of one? No. Not that, because among the bodies kept cool below some, maybe, were his homeboys. He would have to concentrate on something else — a night sky, starless, or, better, train tracks. No scenery, no trains, just endless, endless tracks.

They had taken his shirt and laced boots but his pants and army jacket (neither an effective suicide instrument) were hanging in the locker. He only had to get down the hall to the exit door that was never locked after a fire broke out on that floor and a nurse and two patients died. That was the story Crane, the chatterbox orderly, rapidly chewing gum while washing the patient's armpits, had told him, but he believed it was a simple cover story for the staff's smoke breaks. His first escape plan was to knock Crane out when next he came to clean up his soiling. That required loosening the cuffs, and it was too chancy, so he chose another strategy.

Two days earlier, when he was handcuffed in the back-seat of the patrol car, he had swerved his head wildly to see where he was and where he was going. He had never been in this neighborhood. Central City was his territory. Nothing in particular stood out except the violent neon of a diner sign and a huge yard sign for a tiny church: AME Zion. If he succeeded in getting through the fire exit that's where he would head: to Zion. Still, before escape, he would have to get shoes somehow, some way. Walking anywhere in winter without shoes would guarantee his being arrested and back in the ward until he could be sentenced for vagrancy. Interesting law, vagrancy, meaning standing outside or walking without clear purpose anywhere. Carrying a book would help, but being barefoot would contradict "purposefulness" and standing still could prompt a complaint of "loitering." Better than most, he knew that being outside wasn't necessary for legal or illegal disruption. You could be inside, living in your own house for years, and still, men with or without badges but always with guns could force you, your family, your neighbors to pack up and move — with or without shoes. Twenty years ago, as a four-year-old, he had a pair, though the sole of one flapped with every step. Residents of fifteen houses had been ordered to leave their little neighborhood on the edge of town. Twenty-four hours, they were told, or else. "Else" meaning "die." It was early morning when the warnings came, so the balance of the day was confusion, anger, and packing. By nightfall most were pulling out — on wheels if available, on foot if not. Yet, in spite of the threats from men, both hooded and not, and pleadings from neighbors, one elderly man named Crawford sat on his porch steps and refused to vacate. Elbows on knees, hands clasped, chewing tobacco, he waited the whole night. Just after dawn at the twenty-fourth hour he was beaten to death with pipes and rifle butts and tied to the oldest magnolia tree in the county — the one that grew in his own yard. Maybe it was loving that tree which, he used to brag, his great-grandmother had planted, that made him so stubborn. In the dark of night, some of the fleeing neighbors snuck back to untie him and bury him beneath his beloved magnolia. One of the gravediggers told everyone who would listen that Mr. Crawford's eyes had been carved out.

Although shoes were vital for this escape, the patient had none. Four a.m., before sunrise, he managed to loosen the canvas cuffs, unshackle himself, and rip off the hospital gown. He put on his army pants and jacket and crept shoeless down the hall. Except for the weeping from the room next to the fire exit, all was quiet — no squeak of an orderly's shoes or smothered giggles, and no smell of cigarette smoke. The hinges groaned when he opened the door and the cold hit him like a hammer.

The iced iron of the fire escape steps was so painful he jumped over the railing to sink his feet into the warmer snow on the ground. Maniac moonlight doing the work of absent stars matched his desperate frenzy, lighting his hunched shoulders and footprints left in the snow. He had his service medal in his pocket but no change, so it never occurred to him to look for a phone booth to call Lily. He wouldn't have anyway, not only because of their chilly parting, but also because it would shame him to need her now — a barefoot escapee from the nuthouse. Holding his collar tight at his throat, avoiding shoveled pavement for curb snow, he ran the six blocks as quickly as hospital drug residue would let him to the parsonage of AME Zion, a small two-story clapboard. The steps to the porch were thoroughly cleared of snow, but the house was dark. He knocked — hard, he thought, considering how stiff his hands were, but not threatening like the *bam-bam* of a citizens' group, or a mob or the police. Insistence paid off; a light came on and the door opened a slit, then wider, revealing a gray-haired man in a flannel robe, holding his glasses and frowning at the impudence of a pre-dawn visitor.

He wanted to say "Good morning," or "Excuse me," but his body shook violently like a victim of Saint Vitus's dance and his teeth chattered so uncontrollably he could not make a sound. The man at the door took in the full measure of his shaking visitor, then stepped back to let him in.

"Jean! Jean!" He turned to direct his voice up the stairs before motioning the visitor inside. "Good Lord," he mumbled, pushing the door closed. "You a mess."

He tried to smile and failed.

"My name is Locke, Reverend John Locke. Yours?"

"Frank, sir. Frank Money."

"You from down the street? At that hospital?"

Frank nodded while stamping his feet and trying to rub life back into his fingers.

Reverend Locke grunted. "Have a seat," he said, then, shaking his head, added, "You lucky, Mr. Money. They sell a lot of bodies out of there."

"Bodies?" Frank sank down on the sofa, only vaguely caring or wondering what the man was talking about.

"Uh-huh. To the medical school."

"They sell dead bodies? What for?"

"Well, you know, doctors need to work on the dead poor so they can help the live rich."

"John, stop." Jean Locke came down the stairs, tightening the belt of her robe. "That's just foolishness."

"This is my wife," said Locke. "And while she's sweet as honey, she's often wrong."

"Hello, ma'am. I'm sorry to . . ." Still shivering, Frank stood.

She cut him off. "No need for that. Keep your seat," she said and disappeared into the kitchen.

Frank did as told. Except for the absence of wind, the house was hardly less chilly than outside, and the plastic slipcovers stretched taut over the sofa did not help.

"Sorry if the house is too cold for you." Locke noticed Frank's trembling lips. "We accustomed to rain around here, not snow. Where you from, anyway?"

"Central City."

Locke groaned as though that explained everything. "You looking to get back there?"

"No, sir. I'm on my way south."

"Well how'd you end up in the hospital 'stead of jail? That's where most barefoot, half-dressed folks go."

"The blood, I guess. A lot of it running down my face."

"How'd it get there?"

"I don't know."

"You don't remember?"

"No. Just the noise. Loud. Real loud." Frank rubbed his forehead. "Maybe I was in a fight?" He put the question as though the Reverend might know why he had been bound and sedated for two days.

Reverend Locke gave him a worried glance. Not nervous, just worried. "They must have thought you was dangerous. If you was just sick they'd never let you in. Where exactly you headed, brother?" He was still standing with his hands behind his back.

"Georgia, sir. If I can make it."

"You don't say. That's quite a ways. Does Brother Money have any?" Locke smiled at his own wit.

"Had some when they picked me up," Frank answered. There was nothing in his pants pocket now but his army medal. And he could not remember how much Lily had handed him. Just her turned-down lips and unforgiving eyes.

"But it's gone now, right?" Locke squinted. "Police looking for you?"

"No," said Frank. "No, sir. They just hustled me up and put me in the crazy ward." He cupped his hands before his mouth and breathed on them. "I don't think they brought any charges."

"You wouldn't know it if they did."

Jean Locke returned with a basin of cold water. "Put your feet in here, son. It's cold but you don't want them to heat up too fast."

Frank sank his feet into the water, sighing. "Thanks."

"What'd they pull him in for? The police, I mean." Jean put the question to her husband, who shrugged.

What indeed. Other than that B-29 roar, exactly what he was doing to attract police attention was long gone. He couldn't explain it to himself, let alone to a gentle couple offering help. If he wasn't in a fight was he peeing on the sidewalk? Hollering curses at some passerby, some schoolchildren? Was he banging his head on a wall or hiding behind bushes in somebody's backyard?

"I must have been acting up," he said. "Something like that." He truly could not remember. Had he thrown himself on the ground at the sudden sound of backfire? Perhaps he started a fight with a stranger or started weeping before trees — apologizing to them for acts he had never committed. What he did remember was that as soon as Lily shut the door behind him, in spite of the seriousness of his mission his anxiety became unmanageable. He bought a few shots to steady himself for the long trip. When he left the bar, anxiety did leave but so did sanity. Back was the free-floating rage, the self-loathing disguised as somebody else's fault. And the memories that had ripened at Fort Lawton, from where, no sooner than discharged, he had begun to wander. When he disembarked, he thought to send a telegram home, since no one in Lotus owned a telephone. But along with the telephone operators' strike the telegraph people were striking too. On a two-cent postcard, he wrote, "I am back safe. See you all soon." "Soon" never arrived because he didn't want to go home without his "homeboys." He was far too alive to stand before Mike's folks or Stuff's. His easy breath and unscathed self would be an insult to them. And whatever lie he cooked up about how bravely they died, he could not blame their resentment. Besides, he hated Lotus. Its unforgiving population, its isolation, and especially its indifference to the future were tolerable only if his buddies were there with him.

"How long you been back?" Reverend Locke was still standing. His face softened.

Frank raised his head. "A year about."

Locke scratched his chin and was about to speak when Jean came back with a cup and a plate of soda crackers. "It's just hot water with lots of salt in it," she said. "Drink it up, but slowly. I'll get you a blanket."

Frank sipped twice and then gulped down the rest. When Jean brought more, she said, "Son, dip the crackers in the liquid. They'll go down better."

"Jean," said Locke, "look and see what's in the poor box."

"He needs shoes too, John."

There were none to spare, so they put four pair of socks and some ripped galoshes next to the sofa.

"Get some sleep, brother. You got a rocky journey ahead and I don't just mean Georgia."

Frank fell asleep between a wool blanket and plastic slipcovers and dreamed a dream dappled with body parts. He woke in militant sunlight to the smell of toast. It took a while, longer than it should have, to register where he was. The residue of two days' hospital drugging was leaving, but slowly. Wherever he was, he was grateful the sun's dazzle did not hurt his head. He sat up and noticed socks folded neatly on the rug like broken feet. Then he heard murmurs from another room. As he stared at the socks, the immediate past came into focus: the hospital escape, the freezing run, finally Reverend Locke and his wife. So he was back in the real world when Locke came in and asked how three hours of sleep felt.

"Good. I feel fine," said Frank.

Locke showed him to the bathroom and placed shaving kit and hairbrush on the sink's ledge. Shod and cleaned up, he rummaged in his pants pockets to see if the orderlies had missed anything, a quarter, a dime, but his CIB medal was the only thing they had left him. The money Lily had given him, of course, was gone as well. Frank sat down at the enamel-topped table and ate a breakfast of oatmeal and over-buttered toast. In the center of the table lay eight one-dollar bills and a wash of coins. It could have been a poker pot, except it was surely far more hard-won: dimes slipped from small coin purses; nickels reluctantly given up by children who had other (sweeter) plans for them; the dollar bills representing the generosity of a whole family.

"Seventeen dollars," said Locke. "That's more than enough for a bus ticket to Portland and then on to somewhere near Chicago. Still it sure won't get you to Georgia, but when you get to Portland, here's what you do."

He instructed Frank to get in touch with a Reverend Jessie Maynard, pastor of a Baptist church, and that he would call ahead and tell him to look out for another one.

"Another one?"

"Well, you not the first by a long shot. An integrated army is integrated misery. You all go fight, come back, they treat you like dogs. Change that. They treat dogs better."

Frank stared at him, but didn't say anything. The army hadn't treated him so bad. It wasn't their fault he went ape every now and then. As a matter of fact the discharge doctors had been thoughtful and kind, telling him the craziness would leave in time. They knew all about it, but assured him it would pass. Just stay away from alcohol, they said. Which he didn't. Couldn't. Until he met Lily.

Locke handed Frank a flap torn from an envelope with Maynard's address and told him that Maynard had a big congregation and could offer more help than his own small flock.

Jean had packed six sandwiches, some cheese, some bologna, and three oranges into a grocery bag. She handed it to him along with a watch cap. Frank put on the cap, thanked her and, peering into the bag, asked, "How long a trip is it?"

"Don't matter," said Locke. "You'll be grateful for every bite since you won't be able to sit down at any bus stop counter. Listen here, you from Georgia and you been in a desegregated army and maybe you think up North is way different from down South. Don't believe it and don't count on it. Custom is just as real as law and can be just as dangerous. Come on, now. I'll drive you."

Frank stood at the door, while the Reverend retrieved his coat and car keys.

"Good-bye, Mrs. Locke. I do thank you."

"Stay safe, son," she answered, patting his shoulder.

At the ticket window, Locke converted the coins into paper money and bought Frank's ticket. Before joining the line at the Greyhound door, Frank noticed a police car cruising by. He knelt as though buckling his galoshes. When the danger passed he stood, then turned to Reverend Locke and held out his hand. As the men shook hands they held each other's eyes, saying nothing and everything, as though "good-bye" meant what it once did: God be with you.

There were very few passengers, yet Frank dutifully sat in the last seat, trying to shrink his six-foot-three-inch body and holding the sandwich bag close. From the windows, through the fur of snow, the landscape became more melancholy when the sun successfully brightened the quiet trees, unable to speak without their leaves. The lonesome-looking houses reshaped the snow, while a child's wagon here and there held mounds of it. Only the trucks stuck in driveways looked alive. As he mused about what it might be like in those houses, he could imagine nothing at all. So, as was often the case when he was alone and sober, whatever the surroundings, he saw a boy pushing his entrails back in, holding them in his palms like a fortune-teller's globe shattering with bad news; or he heard a boy with only the bottom half of his face intact, the lips calling mama. And he was stepping over them, around them, to stay alive, to keep his own face from dissolving, his own colorful guts under that oh-so-thin sheet of flesh. Against the black and white of that winter landscape, blood red took center stage. They never went away, these pictures. Except with Lily. He chose not to think of this trip as a breakup. A pause, he hoped. Yet it was hard to ignore what living with her had become: a tired cruelty laced her voice and the buzz of her disappointment defined the silence. Sometimes Lily's face seemed to morph into the front of a jeep — relentless headlight eyes, a bright scouring above a grill-like smile. Strange, how she had changed. Remembering what he loved about her, the slight paunch, the backs of her knees, and her knockout beautiful face, it was as though someone had redrawn her as a cartoon. It couldn't all be his fault, could it? Didn't he smoke outside the apartment building? Put more than half his pay on the dresser for her to spend any way she wanted? Do her the courtesy of raising the toilet seat — which she took as an insult. And although he was amazed and amused by the female paraphernalia that hung from the bathroom door or cluttered cabinets, sink ledges, and every available space — douche bags, enema attachments, bottles of Massingill, Lydia Pinkham, Kotex, Neet hair removal, facial creams, mud-packs, curlers, lotions, deodorants — he never touched or questioned them. Yes, he sat on occasion for hours in the quiet — numb, unwilling to talk. Yes, he regularly lost the few odd jobs he'd managed to secure. And while sometimes being near her made it hard to breathe, he was not at all sure he could live without her. It wasn't just the lovemaking, entering what he called the kingdom between her legs. When he lay with the girl-weight of her arm on his chest, the nightmares folded away and he could sleep. When he woke up with her, his first thought was not the welcome sting of whiskey. Most important, he was no longer attracted to other women — whether they were openly flirting or on display for their own private pleasure. He didn't rank them against Lily; he simply saw them as people. Only with Lily did the pictures fade, move behind a screen in his brain, pale but waiting, waiting and accusing. Why didn't you hurry? If you had gotten there sooner you could have helped him. You could have pulled him behind the hill the way you did Mike. And all of that killing you did afterward? Women running, dragging children along. And that old one-legged man on a crutch hobbling at the edge of the road so as not to slow down the other, swifter ones? You blew a hole in his head because you believed it would make up for the frosted urine on Mike's pants and avenge the lips calling mama. Did it? Did it work? And the girl. What did she ever do to deserve what happened to her? All unasked questions multiplying like mold in the shadows of the photographs he saw. Before Lily. Before seeing her stand on a chair, stretch, reach up to a high shelf in her cupboard to get the can of Calumet she needed for the meal she was preparing for him. Their first. He should have jumped up, pulled the tin from the shelf. But he did not. He could not take his eyes away from the backs of her knees. As she stretched, her dress of a soft cottony flowered fabric rose up, exposing that seldom noticed, ooo-so-vulnerable flesh. And for a reason he still did not understand, he began to cry. Love plain, simple, and so fast it shattered him.

There was no love from Jessie Maynard in Portland. Help, yes. But the contempt was glacial. The Reverend was devoted to the needy, apparently, but only if they were properly clothed and not a young, hale, and very tall veteran. He kept Frank on the back porch near the driveway, where a Rocket 98 Oldsmobile lurked, and smiled knowingly as he said, by way of apology, "My daughters are inside the house." It was an insult tax levied on the supplicant for an overcoat, sweater and two ten-dollar bills. Enough to get to Chicago and maybe halfway to Georgia. Still, hostile as he was, Reverend Maynard gave him helpful information for his journey. From Green's travelers' book he copied out some addresses and names of rooming houses, hotels where he would not be turned away.

Frank shoved the list in the pocket of the coat the Reverend gave him and, beyond Maynard's view, stuffed the bills inside his socks. As he walked to the train station his nervousness about whether he would have another incident — uncontrollable, suspicious, destructive, and illegal — was shrinking. Besides, sometimes he could tell when a break was coming. It happened the first time when he boarded a bus near Fort Lawton, discharge papers intact. He was quiet, just sitting next to a brightly dressed woman. Her flowered skirt was a world's worth of color, her blouse a loud red. Frank watched the flowers at the hem of her

17

skirt blackening and her red blouse draining of color until it was white as milk. Then everybody, everything. Outside the window — trees, sky, a boy on a scooter, grass, hedges. All color disappeared and the world became a black-and-white movie screen. He didn't yell then because he thought something bad was happening to his eyes. Bad, but fixable. He wondered if this was how dogs or cats or wolves saw the world. Or was he becoming color-blind? At the next stop he got off and walked toward a Chevron station, its black flames shooting out from the V. He wanted to get into the bathroom, pee, and look in the mirror to see if he had an eye infection, but the sign on the door stopped him. He relieved himself in the shrubbery behind the station, annoyed and a little frightened by the colorless landscape. The bus was about to pull away, but stopped to let him reboard. He got off at the last stop — the bus station in the same city where he had disembarked to the sight of singing high school girls welcoming the war-weary vets. Out in the street in front of the bus station the sun hurt him. Its mean light drove him to look for shade. And there, under a northern oak, the grass turned green. Relieved, he knew he wouldn't shout, smash anything, or accost strangers. That came later when, whatever the world's palette, his shame and its fury exploded. Now, if the signs of draining color gave notice, he would have time to hurry up and hide. Thus, whenever a smattering of color returned, he was pleased to know he wasn't going color-blind and the horrible pictures might fade. Confidence restored, he could abide a day and a half on a train to Chicago without incident.

Signaled by a redcap, he entered a passenger car, pushed through the green separation curtain, and found a window seat. The train's rocking and the singing rails soothed him into a rare sleep that was so sound he missed the beginning of the riot, but not its end. He woke to the sobbing of a young woman being comforted by white-jacketed waiters. One of them nestled a pillow behind her head; another gave her a stack of linen napkins for her tears and the blood pouring from her nose. Next to her, looking away, was her silent, seething husband — his face a skull of shame and its partner, rigid anger.

When a waiter passed by, Frank touched his arm, asking, "What happened?" He pointed to the couple.

"You didn't see that?"

"No. What was it?"

"That there is the husband. He got off at Elko to buy some coffee or something back there." He jerked his thumb over his shoulder. "The owner or customers or both kicked him out. Actually. Put their feet in his butt and knocked him down, kicked some more, and when his lady came to help, she got a rock thrown in her face. We got them back in the car, but the crowd kept the yelling up till we pulled away. Look," he said. "See that?" He pointed to egg yolks, not sliding now but stuck like phlegm to the window.

"Anybody report to the conductor?" Frank asked him.

"You crazy?"

"Probably. Say, you know a good place to eat and get some sleep in Chicago? I got a list here. You know anything about these places?"

The waiter took off his glasses, replaced them and scanned Reverend Maynard's list.

The waiter pursed his lips. "To eat go to Booker's diner," he said. "It's close to the station. For sleeping the YMCA is always a good idea. It's on Wabash. These hotels and what they call tourist homes can cost you a pretty penny and they might not let you in with those raggedy galoshes on your feet."

"Thanks," said Frank. "Glad to hear they got high standards."

The waiter chuckled. "You want a shot? I got some Johnnie Red in my case." C. TAYLOR was printed on his name tag.

"Yeah. Oh, yeah."

Frank's taste buds, uninterested in cheese sandwiches or oranges, came alive at the mention of whiskey. Just a shot. Just enough to settle and sweeten the world. No more.

The wait seemed long and just when Frank was convinced the man had forgotten, Taylor returned with a coffee cup, saucer and napkin. An inch of Scotch trembled invitingly in the thick white cup.

"Here you go," said Taylor, then he rocked along the aisle to the sway of the train.

The abused couple whispered to each other, she softly, pleadingly, he with urgency. He will beat her when they get home, thought Frank. And who wouldn't? It's one thing to be publicly humiliated. A

20

man could move on from that. What was intolerable was the witness of a woman, a wife, who not only saw it, but had dared to try to rescue — rescue! — him. He couldn't protect himself and he couldn't protect her either, as the rock in her face proved. She would have to pay for that broken nose. Over and over again.

With his head back on the window frame he napped a bit following the cup of Scotch and woke when he heard someone taking the seat next to him. Odd. There were several empty seats throughout the car. He turned and, more amused than startled, examined his seat partner — a small man wearing a wide-brimmed hat. His pale blue suit sported a long jacket and balloon trousers. His shoes were white with unnaturally pointed toes. The man stared ahead. Ignored, Frank leaned back to the window to pick up his nap. As soon as he did, the zoot-suited man got up and disappeared down the aisle. No indentation was left in the leather seat.

Passing through freezing, poorly washed scenery, Frank tried to redecorate it, mind-painting giant slashes of purple and X's of gold on hills, dripping yellow and green on barren wheat fields. Hours of trying and failing to recolor the western landscape agitated him, but by the time he stepped off the train he was calm enough. The station noise was so abrasive, though, that he reached for a sidearm. None was there, of course, so he leaned against a steel support until the panic died down.

An hour later he was scooping up navy beans and buttering corn bread. Taylor, the waiter, had been right. Booker's was not only a good and cheap place to eat, but its company — diners, counter help, waitresses, and a loud argumentative cook — was welcoming and high-spirited. Laborers and the idle, mothers and street women, all ate and drank with the ease of family in their own kitchens. It was that quick, down-home friendliness that led Frank to talk freely to the man on the stool next to his who volunteered his name.

"Watson. Billy Watson." He held out his hand.

"Frank Money."

"Where you from, Frank?"

"Aw, man. Korea, Kentucky, San Diego, Seattle, Georgia. Name it I'm from it."

"You looking to be from here too?"

"No. I'm headed on back to Georgia."

"Georgia?" the waitress shouted. "I got people in Macon. No good memories about that place. We hid in an abandoned house for half a year."

"Hid from what? White sheets?"

"Naw. The rent man."

"Same thing."

"Why him?"

"Oh, please. It was 1938."

Up and down the counter there was laughter, loud and knowing. Some began to compete with stories of their own deprived life in the thirties.

Me and my brother slept in a freight car for a month.

Where was it headed?

Away, was all we knew.

You ever sleep in a coop the chickens wouldn't enter?

Aw, man, shut up. We lived in a ice house.

Where was the ice?

22

We ate it.

Get out!

I slept on so many floors, first time I saw a bed I thought it was a coffin.

You ever eat dandelions?

In soup, they good.

Hog guts. They call it something fancy now, but butchers used to throw them out or give them to us.

Feet too. Necks. All offal.

Hush. You ruining my business.

When the boasts and laughter died down, Frank retrieved Maynard's list.

"You know any of these places? I was told the Y was best."

Billy scanned the addresses and frowned. "Forget that," he said. "Come on home with me. Stay over. Meet my family. You can't leave tonight anyway."

"True," said Frank.

"I'll get you back to the station on time tomorrow. You taking a bus south or the train? Bus is cheaper."

"Train, Billy. Long as there're porters, that's the way I want to travel."

"They sure make good money. Four hundred, five a month. Plus tips."

They walked all the way to Billy's house.

"We'll buy you some decent shoes in the morning," said Billy. "And maybe a stop at the Goodwill, okay?"

Frank laughed. He had forgotten how raggedy he looked. Chicago, braced by wind and a smug twilight sky, was full of strutting, well-dressed pedestrians moving quickly — as though meeting a deadline somewhere down sidewalks wider than any Lotus road. By the time they left downtown and entered Billy's neighborhood, night was on its way.

"Say hello to my wife, Arlene, and this is our little man, Thomas."

Frank thought Arlene pretty enough for the stage. Her pompadour crowned a high, smooth forehead over fierce brown eyes.

"You all want supper?" Arlene asked.

"No," Billy said. "We ate already."

"Good." Arlene was getting ready for her night shift at the metal factory. She kissed Thomas on the top of his head as he sat at the kitchen table reading a book.

Billy and Frank leaned over the coffee table, rearranging its doodads for space to play tonk, talk, and nurse beer.

"What work you do?" asked Frank.

"Steel," said Billy. "But we on strike now, so I join the line at the agency and take any daywork I can get."

Earlier, when Billy introduced his son to Frank, the boy had lifted his left arm to shake hands. Frank noticed the right one sagging at his side. Now, shuffling the deck, he asked what happened to his son's arm. Billy arranged his hands in rifle position. "Drive-by cop," he said. "He had a cap pistol. Eight years old, running up and down the sidewalk pointing it. Some redneck rookie thought his dick was underappreciated by his brother cops."

"You can't just shoot a kid," said Frank.

"Cops shoot anything they want. This here's a mob city. Arlene went a little crazy in the emergency room.

24

They threw her out twice. But it turned out all right in the end. The bad arm kept him off the streets and in the classroom. He's a math whiz. Wins competitions all over. Scholarships pouring in."

"So the boy cop did him a favor."

"No. No, no, no. Jesus stepped in and did that. He said, 'Hold on there, Mr. Police Guy. Don't hurt the least of mine. He who harms the least of mine disturbs the tranquillity of my mind.'"

Beautiful, thought Frank. Bible stuff works every time every place — except the fire zone. "Jesus. Jesus!" That's what Mike said. Stuff yelled it too. "Jesus, God Almighty, I'm fucked, Frank, Jesus, help me."

The math whiz had no objection to sleeping on the sofa and letting his father's new friend have his bed. Frank approached him in the boy's bedroom, saying, "Thanks, buddy."

"My name is Thomas," said the boy.

"Oh, okay, Thomas. I hear you good at math."

"I'm good at everything."

"Like what?"

"Civics, geography, English . . ." His voice trailed off as though he could have cited many more subjects he was good at.

"You'll go far, son."

"And I'll go deep."

Frank laughed at the impudence of the eleven-year-old. "What sport you play?" he asked, thinking maybe the boy needed a little humility. But Thomas gave him a look so cold Frank was embarrassed. "I mean . . ."

"I know what you mean," he said and, as a counterpoint or afterthought, he looked Frank up and down and said, "You shouldn't drink."

"Got that right."

A short silence followed while Thomas placed a folded blanket on top of a pillow, tucking both under his dead arm. At the bedroom door he turned to Frank. "Were you in the war?"

"I was."

"Did you kill anybody?"

"Had to."

"How did it feel?"

"Bad. Real bad."

"That's good. That it made you feel bad. I'm glad."

"How come?"

"It means you're not a liar."

"You are deep, Thomas." Frank smiled. "What you want to be when you grow up?"

Thomas turned the knob with his left hand and opened the door. "A man," he said and left.

Settling down into darkness shaped by the moonlit edges of the window shades, Frank hoped this fragile sobriety, maintained so far without Lily, would not subject him to those same dreams. But the mare always showed up at night, never beating her hooves in daylight. The taste of Scotch on the train, two beers hours later — he'd had no problem limiting himself. Sleep came fairly soon, with only one image of fingered feet — or was it toe-tipped hands? But after a few hours of dreamlessness, he woke to the sound of a click like the squeeze of a trigger from a gun minus ammo. Frank sat up. Nothing stirred. Then he saw the outline of the small man, the one from the train, his wide-brimmed hat unmistakable in the frame of light at the window. Frank reached for the bedside lamp. Its glow revealed the same little man in the pale blue zoot suit.

"Hey! Who the hell are you? What you want?" Frank rose from the bed and moved toward the figure. After three steps the zoot-suited man disappeared.

Frank went back to bed, thinking that particular living dream was not all that bad compared to others he'd had. No dogs or birds eating the remains of his comrades, like the hallucination he'd had once while sitting on a bench in the city park's rose garden. This one was comic, in a way. He had heard about those suits, but never saw anybody wearing one. If they were the signals of manhood, he would have preferred a loincloth and some white paint artfully smeared on forehead and cheeks. Holding a spear, of course. But the zoot-suiters chose another costume: wide shoulders, wide-brimmed hats, watch chains, pants ballooned up from narrow cuffs beyond the waist to the chest. It had been enough of a fashion statement to interest riot cops on each coast.

Damn! He didn't want some new dream ghost for company. Unless it was a sign trying to tell him something. Was it about his sister? The letter said, "She be dead." Meaning she's alive but sick, very sick, and obviously there was no one to help her. If the letter writer, Sarah, couldn't help nor her boss either, well, she must be withering away far from home. Parents dead, one of lung disease, another of a stroke. Strike the grandparents, Salem and Lenore. Neither one was capable of travel, assuming they'd even be interested. Maybe that was the reason no Russian-made bullet had blown his head off while everybody else he was close to died over there. Maybe his life had been preserved for Cee, which was only fair since she had been his original caring-for, a selflessness without gain or emotional profit. Even before she could walk he'd taken care of her. The first word she spoke was "Fwank." Two of her baby teeth were hidden in the kitchen matchbox along with his lucky marbles and the broken watch they had found on the riverbank. Cee suffered no bruise or cut he had not tended. The only thing he could not do for her was wipe the sorrow, or was it panic, from her eyes when he enlisted. He tried to tell her the army was the only solution. Lotus was suffocating, killing him and his two best friends. They all agreed. Frank assured himself Cee would be okay.

She wasn't.

Arlene was still asleep, so Billy cooked breakfast for the three of them.

"What time is her shift over?"

Billy poured pancake batter into a hot frying pan. "She is on the eleven to seven. She'll be up soon, but I won't see her until evening."

"How come?" Frank was curious. The rules and accommodations normal families made were a fascination that did not rise to the level of envy.

"After I walk Thomas to school, I'll be late in line at the agency because you and me going shopping. By that time all the best day jobs will be taken already. I'll see what leavings I can get. But shopping first. You look like . . ."

"Don't say it."

He didn't have to. And the woman at the Goodwill store didn't either. She led them to a table of folded clothes and nodded toward a rack of hanging coats and jackets. Choosing was quick. Every item was clean, pressed and organized for size. Even the body odor of the previous owner was mild. The store had a dressing room where a bum or a respectable family man could change clothes and toss the worn ones in a bin. Suitably dressed, Frank felt proud enough to take his medal from his army pants and pin it to his breast pocket.

"Okay," said Billy. "Now for some grown man's shoes. Thorn McAn or do you want Florsheim?"

"Neither. I ain't going to a dance. Work shoes."

"Got it. You got enough money?"

"Yep."

The police would have thought so too, but during the random search outside the shoe store they just patted pockets, not the inside of work boots. Of the two other men facing the wall, one had his switchblade confiscated, the other a dollar bill. All four lay their hands on the hood of the patrol car parked at the curb. The younger officer noticed Frank's medal.

"Korea?"

"Yes, sir."

"Hey, Dick. They're vets."

"Yeah?"

"Yeah. Look." The officer pointed to Frank's service medal.

"Go on. Get lost, pal."

The police incident was not worth comment so Frank and Billy walked off in silence. Then they stopped at a street vendor's tray to buy a wallet.

"You wearing a suit now. You can't be reaching in your shoe like a kid every time you want a pack of gum." Billy punched Frank's arm.

"How much?" Billy examined the wallets on display.

"A quarter."

"What? A loaf of bread ain't but fifteen cents."

"So?" The vendor stared at his customer. "Wallets last longer. You in or you out?"

Following the purchase Billy accompanied Frank all the way to Booker's diner, where they leaned against the plate glass, shook hands, promised to visit each other, and parted.

Frank had coffee and flirted with the counter waitress from Macon until it was time to board the southbound rails that would take him to Georgia and Cee and who knew what else.

CHAPTER
THREE

Mama was pregnant when we walked out of Bandera County, Texas. Three or maybe four families had trucks or cars and loaded all they could. But remember, nobody could load their land, their crops, their stock. Is somebody going to feed the hogs or let them go wild? What about that patch behind the shed? It needs tilling in case it rains. Most families, like mine, walked for miles until Mr. Gardener came back for a few more of us after dropping his own people at the state line. We had to leave our wheelbarrow full of stuff in order to pile into his car, trading goods for speed. Mama cried, but the baby she carried was more important than kettles, canning jars, and bedding. She contented herself with a basket of clothes held on her knees. Pap carried a few tools in a sack and the reins of Stella, our horse that we would never see again. After Mr. Gardener took us as far as he could we walked some more. The sole of my shoe flapped until Pap tied it up with his own shoelace. Twice, draymen let us ride in their wagon bed. Talk about tired. Talk about hungry. I have eaten trash in jail, Korea, hospitals, at table, and from certain garbage cans. Nothing, however, compares to the leftovers at food pantries. Write about that, why don't you? I remember standing in line at Church of the Redeemer waiting for a tin plate of dry, hard cheese already showing green, pickled pigs' feet — its vinegar soaking stale biscuits.

It was there that Mama heard the woman ahead of her explain to the volunteer how to spell and pronounce her name. Mama said it was the sweetest thing and the sound of the name was like music amid the argue and heat of the crowd. Weeks later, when her baby, delivered on a mattress in Reverend Bailey's church basement, turned out to be a girl, Mama named her Ycidra, taking care to pronounce all three syllables. Of course, she waited the nine days before naming, lest death notice fresh life and eat it. Everybody but Mama calls her "Cee." I always thought it was nice, how she thought about the name, treasured it. As for me, no such memories. I am named Frank after my father's brother. Luther is my father's name, Ida my mother's. The crazy part is our last name. Money. Of which we had none.

You don't know what heat is until you cross the border from Texas to Louisiana in the summer. You can't come up with words that catch it.

Trees give up. Turtles cook in their shells. Describe that if you know how.

CHAPTER
FOUR

A mean grandmother is one of the worst things a girl could have. Mamas are supposed to spank and rule you so you grow up knowing right from wrong. Grandmothers, even when they've been hard on their own children, are forgiving and generous to the grandchildren. Ain't that so?

Cee stood up in the zinc tub and took a few dripping steps to the sink. She filled a bucket from the faucet, poured it into the warming tub water, and sat back down in it. She wanted to linger in cool water while a softly suffering afternoon light encouraged her thoughts to tumble. Regrets, excuses, righteousness, false memory, and future plans mixed together or stood like soldiers in line. Well, that's the way grandmothers should be, she thought, but for little Ycidra Money it wasn't like that at all. Because Mama and Pap worked from before sunrise until dark, they never knew that Miss Lenore poured water instead of milk over the shredded wheat Cee and her brother ate for breakfast. Nor that when they had stripes and welts on their legs they were cautioned to lie, to say they got them by playing out by the stream where brambles and huckleberry thorns grew. Even their grandfather Salem was silent. Frank said it was because he was scared Miss Lenore would leave him the way his first two wives did. Lenore, who had collected a five-hundred-dollar life-insurance payment upon her first husband's death, was a serious catch for an old, unemployable man. Besides, she had a Ford and owned her house. She was so valuable to Salem Money he never made a sound when the salt pork was halved for the two of them and all the children got was its flavor. Well, yes, the grandparents were doing them a big favor letting some homeless relatives live in their house after the family got run out of Texas. Lenore took it as a very bad sign for Cee's future that she was born on the road. Decent women, she said, delivered babies at home, in a bed attended to by good Christian women who knew what to do. Although only street women, prostitutes, went to hospitals when they got pregnant, at least they had a roof overhead when their baby came. Being born in the street — or the gutter, as she usually put it — was prelude to a sinful, worthless life.

Lenore's house was big enough for two, maybe three, but not for grandparents plus Pap, Mama, Uncle Frank and two children — one a howling baby. Over the years, the discomfort of the crowded house increased, and Lenore, who believed herself superior to everybody else in Lotus, chose to focus her resentment on the little girl born "in the street." A frown creased her every glance when the girl entered, her lips turned down at every drop of a spoon, trip on the door saddle, a loosening braid. Most of all was the murmur of "gutter child" as she walked away from a failing that was always on display from her step-granddaughter. During those years Cee slept with her parents on the floor, on a thin pallet hardly better than the pine slats underneath. Uncle Frank used two chairs put together; young Frank slept on the back porch, on the slanty wooden swing, even when it rained. Her parents, Luther and Ida, worked two jobs each — Ida picking cotton or working other crops in the day and sweeping lumber shacks in the evening; Luther and Uncle Frank were field-workers for two planters in nearby Jeffrey and very happy to have the jobs other men had abandoned. Most of the young ones had enlisted in the war and when it was over didn't come back to work cotton, peanuts, or lumber. Then Uncle Frank enlisted too. He got in the navy as a cook and was glad about that because he didn't have to handle explosives. But his ship sank anyway and Miss Lenore hung the gold star in the window as though she, and not one of Salem's ex-wives, was the honorable, patriotic mother who had lost a son. Ida's job at the lumber yard gave her a lethal asthma but it paid off because at the end of those three years with Lenore they were able to rent a place from Old Man Shepherd, who drove in from Jeffrey every Saturday morning to collect the rent.

Cee remembered the relief and the pride they all took in having their own garden and their own laying hens. The Moneys had enough of it to feel at home in this place where neighbors could finally offer friendship instead of pity. Everybody in the neighborhood, except Lenore, was stern but quickly open-handed. If someone had an abundance of peppers or collards, they insisted

Ida take them. There was okra, fish fresh from the creek, a bushel of corn, all kinds of food that should not go to waste. One woman sent her husband over to shore up their slanted porch steps. They were generous to strangers. An outsider passing through was welcomed — even, or especially, if he was running from the law. Like that man, bloody and scared, the one they washed up, fed and led away on a mule. It was nice having their own house where they could let Mr. Haywood put them on his monthly list of people who needed supplies from the general store in Jeffrey. Sometimes he would bring back comic books, bubblegum and peppermint balls free, for the children. Jeffrey had sidewalks, running water, stores, a post office, a bank and a school. Lotus was separate, with no sidewalks or indoor plumbing, just fifty or so houses and two churches, one of which churchwomen used for teaching reading and arithmetic. Cee thought it would have been better if there were more books to read — not just *Aesop's Fables* and a book of Bible passages for young people — and much much better if she had been permitted to attend the school in Jeffrey.

That, she believed, was the reason she ran off with a rat. If she hadn't been so ignorant living in a no-count, not-even-a-town place with only chores, church-school, and nothing else to do, she would have known better. Watched, watched, watched by every grown-up from sunrise to sunset and ordered about by not only Lenore but every adult in town. Come here, girl, didn't nobody teach you how to sew? Yes, ma'am. Then why is your hem hanging like that? Yes, ma'am. I mean no, ma'am.

Is that lipstick on your mouth? No, ma'am. What then? Cherries, ma'am, I mean blackberries. I ate some. Cherries, my foot. Wipe your mouth. Come down from that tree, you hear me? Tie your shoes put down that rag doll and pick up a broom uncross your legs go weed that garden stand up straight don't you talk back to me. When Cee and a few other girls reached fourteen and started talking about boys, she was prevented from any real flirtation because of her big brother, Frank. The boys knew she was off-limits because of him. That's why when Frank and his two best friends enlisted and left town, she fell for what Lenore called the first thing she saw wearing belted trousers instead of overalls.

His name was Principal but he called himself Prince. A visitor from Atlanta to his aunt's house, he was a good-looking new face with shiny, thin-soled shoes. All the girls were impressed with his big-city accent and what they believed was his knowledge and wide experience. Cee most of all.

Now, splashing water on her shoulders, she wondered for the umpteenth time why she didn't at least ask the aunt he was visiting why he was sent to the backwoods instead of spending the winter in the big, bad city. But feeling adrift in the space where her brother had been, she had no defense. That's the other side, she thought, of having a smart, tough brother close at hand to take care of and protect you — you are slow to develop your own brain muscle. Besides, Prince loved himself so deeply, so completely, it was impossible to doubt his conviction. So if Prince said she was pretty, she believed him. If he said at fourteen she was a woman, she believed that too. And if he said, I want you for myself, it was Lenore who said, "Not unless y'all are legal." Whatever legal meant. Ycidra didn't even have a birth certificate and the courthouse was over a hundred miles away. So they had Reverend Alsop come over and bless them, write their names in a huge book before walking back to her parents' house. Frank had enlisted, so his bed was where they slept and where the great thing people warned about or giggled about took place. It was not so much painful as dull. Cee thought it would get better later. Better turned out to be simply more, and while the quantity increased, its pleasure lay in its brevity.

There was no job in or around Lotus that Prince allowed himself to take so he took her to Atlanta. Cee looked forward to a shiny life in the city where — after a few weeks of ogling water coming from the turn of a spigot, inside toilets free of flies, streetlights shining longer than the sun and as lovely as fireflies, women in high heels and gorgeous hats trotting to church two, sometimes three times a day, and following the grateful joy and dumbfounded delight of the pretty dress Prince bought her — she learned that Principal had married her for an automobile.

Lenore had bought a used station wagon from Shepherd the rent man and, since Salem couldn't drive, Lenore gave her old Ford to Luther and Ida — with the caution that they give it back if the station wagon broke down. A few times Luther let Prince use the Ford on errands: trips to the post office in Jeffrey for mail to or from wherever Frank was stationed, first Kentucky, then Korea. Once he drove to town for throat medicine for Ida when her breathing problems got worse. His having easy access to the Ford suited everyone because Prince washed away the eternal road dust that floured it, changed plugs and oil, and never gave lifts to the boys who begged to join him in the car. It was natural for Luther to agree to let the couple drive it to Atlanta, since they promised to return it in a few weeks.

Never happened.

She was all alone now, sitting in a zinc tub on a Sunday defying the heat of Georgia's version of spring with cool water while Prince was cruising around with his thin-soled shoes pressing the gas pedal in California or New York, for all she knew. When Prince left her to her own devices, Cee rented a cheaper room on a quiet street, a room with kitchen privileges and use of a washtub. Thelma, who lived in a big apartment upstairs, became a friend and helped her get a job dishwashing at Bobby's Rib House, fusing the friendship with blunt counsel.

"No fool like a country fool. Why don't you go back to your folks?"

"Without the car?" Lord, thought Cee. Lenore had already threatened to have her arrested. When Ida died, Cee traveled by car to the funeral. Bobby had let his fry cook drive her. As pitiful as the funeral was — homemade pine coffin, no flowers except the two branches of honeysuckle she had snatched — nothing was more hurtful than Lenore's name-calling accusations. Thief, fool, hussy; she ought to call the sheriff. When Cee got back to the city, she swore never to go back there. A promise kept, even when Pap died of a stroke a month later.

Ycidra agreed with Thelma about her foolishness, but more than anything she wanted desperately to talk to her brother. Her letters to him were about weather and Lotus gossip. Devious. But she knew that if she could see him, tell him, he would not laugh at her, quarrel, or condemn. He would, as always, protect her from a bad situation. Like the time he, Mike, Stuff, and some other boys were playing softball in a field. Cee sat nearby, leaning on a butternut tree. The boys' game bored her. She glanced at the players intermittently, focused intently on the cherry-red polish she was picking from her nails, hoping to remove it all before Lenore could berate her for "flaunting" her little hussy self. She looked up and saw Frank leaving the plate with his bat, only because others were yelling. "Where you going, man?" "Hey, hey. You out?" He walked slowly away from the field and disappeared into the surrounding trees. Circling, she later learned. Suddenly he was behind the tree she was leaning against, swinging his bat twice into the legs of a man she had not even noticed standing behind her. Mike and the others ran to see what she had not. Then they all ran, Frank dragging her by the arm — not even looking back. She had questions: "What happened? Who was that?" The boys didn't answer. They simply muttered curses. Hours later, Frank explained. The man wasn't from Lotus, he told her, and had been hiding behind the tree, flashing her. When she pressed her brother to define "flashing," and he did so, Cee began to tremble.

40

Frank put one hand on top of her head, the other at her nape. His fingers, like balm, stopped the trembling and the chill that accompanied it. She followed Frank's advice always: recognized poisonous berries, shouted when in snake territory, learned the medicinal uses of spiderwebs. His instructions were specific, his cautions clear.

But he never warned her about rats.

Four barnyard swallows gathered on the lawn outside. Politely equidistant from one another, they peck-searched through blades of drying grass. Then, as if summoned, all four flew up to a pecan tree. Towel wrapped, Cee went to the window and raised it to just below the place where the screen was torn. The quiet seemed to slither, then boom, its weight more theatrical than noise. It was like the quiet of the Lotus house afternoon and evening as she and her brother figured out what to do or talk about. Their parents worked sixteen hours and were hardly there. So they invented escapades, or investigated surrounding territory. Often they sat by the stream, leaning on a lightning-blasted sweet bay tree whose top had been burned off, leaving it with two huge branches below that spread like arms. Even when Frank was with his friends Mike and Stuff, he let her tag along. The four of them were tight, the way family ought to be. She remembered how unwelcome drop-in visits to her grandparents' house were, unless Lenore needed them for chores. Salem was uninspiring since he was mute about everything except his meals. His single enthusiasm, besides food, was playing cards or chess with some other old men. Their parents were so beat by the time they came home from work, any affection they showed was like a razor — sharp, short, and thin. Lenore was the wicked witch. Frank and Cee, like some forgotten Hansel and Gretel, locked hands as they navigated the silence and tried to imagine a future.

Standing at the window, wrapped in the scratchy towel, Cee felt her heart breaking. If Frank were there he would once more touch the top of her head with four fingers, or stroke her nape with his thumb. Don't cry, said the fingers; the welts will disappear. Don't cry; Mama is tired; she didn't mean it. Don't cry, don't cry girl; I'm right here. But he wasn't there or anywhere near. In the photograph he'd sent home, a smiling warrior in a uniform, holding a rifle, he looked as though he belonged to something else, something beyond and unlike Georgia. Months after he was discharged, he sent a two-cent postcard to say where he was living. Cee wrote back:

"Hello brother how are you I am fine. I just got me a ok job in a restaurant but looking for a better one. Write back when you can Yours truly Your sister."

Now she stood, alone; her body, already throwing off whatever good the tub soak had done, beginning to sweat. She toweled the damp under her breasts, then wiped perspiration from her forehead. She raised the window way above the tear in the screen. The swallows were back, bringing with them a light breeze and an odor of sage growing at the edge of the yard. Cee watched, thinking, So this is what they mean in those sad, sweet songs. "When I lost my baby, I almost lost my mind . . ." Except those songs were about lost love. What she felt was bigger than that. She was broken. Not broken up but broken down, down into her separate parts.

Cooled, finally, she unhooked the dress Principal had bought her their second day in Atlanta — not, she learned, from generosity but because he was ashamed of her countrified clothes. He couldn't take her to dinner or a party or to meet his family, he said, in the ugly dress she wore. Yet, after he bought the new one, he had excuse after excuse about why they spent most of the time just driving around, even eating, in the Ford, but never met any of his friends or family.

"Where is your aunt? Shouldn't we go see her?"

"Naw. She don't like me and I don't like her either."

"But if it hadn't been for her we would never have met each other."

"Yeah. Right."

Nevertheless, though nobody saw it, the rayon-silky touch of the dress still pleased her, as did its riot of blue dahlias on a white background. She had never seen a flower-printed dress before. Once dressed, she dragged the tub through the kitchen and out the back door. Slowly, carefully she rationed the bathwater onto the wilted grass, a half bucketful here, a little more there, taking care to let her feet but not her dress get wet.

Gnats buzzed over a bowl of black grapes on the kitchen table. Cee waved them away, rinsed the fruit and sat down to munch them while she thought about her situation: tomorrow was Monday; she had four dollars; rent due at week's end was twice that. Next

Friday she was to be paid eighteen dollars, a bit over three dollars a day. So, eighteen dollars coming in, minus eight going out, left her about fourteen dollars. With that she would have to buy everything a girl needed to be presentable, keep and make progress on her job. Her hope was to move from dishwasher to short-order cook and maybe to waitress who got tips. She had left Lotus with nothing and, except for the new dress, Prince had left her with nothing. She needed soap, underwear, toothbrush, toothpaste, deodorant, another dress, shoes, stockings, jacket, sanitary napkins, and maybe have enough left for a fifteen-cent movie in a balcony seat. Fortunately, at Bobby's she could eat two meals for free. Solution: more work — a second job or a better one.

For that, she needed to see Thelma, her upstairs neighbor. After knocking timidly Cee opened the door and found her friend rinsing dishes at the sink.

"I saw you out there. You think sloshing dirty water is going to green up that yard?" asked Thelma.

"Can't hurt."

"Yes, it can." Thelma wiped her hands. "This is the hottest spring I've seen. Mosquitoes be doing their blood dance the whole night long. All they need is a smell of water."

"Sorry."

"I don't doubt that." Thelma patted her apron pocket for a pack of Camels. Lighting one, she eyed her friend. "That's a pretty dress. Where'd you get it?" They both moved to the living room and plopped down on the sofa.

"Prince bought it for me when we first moved here."

"Prince." Thelma snorted. "You mean Frog. I've seen no-counts by the truckload. Never saw anybody more useless than him. Do you even know where he is?"

"No."

"You want to?"

"No."

"Well thank the Lord for that."

"I need a job, Thelma."

"You got one. Don't tell me you quit Bobby's?"

"No. But I need something better. Better paying. I don't get tips and I have to eat at the restaurant, whether I want to or not."

"Bobby's food is the best. You can't eat anywhere better."

"I know, but I need a real job where I can save. And no, I'm not going back to Lotus."

"Can't fault you for that. Your family is crying-out-loud crazy." Thelma leaned back, curled her tongue into a tube to funnel the smoke.

Cee hated to see her do that, but hid her disgust. "Mean, maybe. Not crazy."

"Oh yeah? Named you Yeidra, didn't they?"

"Thelma?" Cee rested her elbows on her knees and turned pleading eyes to her friend. "Please? Think about it."

"Okay. Okay. Say, matter of fact, you might be in luck. Just so happens I heard about something couple weeks ago when I was in Reba's. Everything worth knowing you can pick up in her beauty shop. Did you know Reverend Smith's wife is pregnant again? Eleven already underfoot and another coming. I know a preacher is a man too, but dear Lord. He should be praying at night instead of . . ."

"Thelma, I mean what did you hear about a job?"

"Oh. Just that a couple in Buckhead — just outside the city — Reba said they need a second."

"A second what?"

"They got a cook-housekeeper, but they want a maid-type person to help the husband. He's a doctor. Nice people."

"You mean like a nurse?"

"No. A helper. I don't know. Bandages and iodine, I guess. His office is in the house, the woman said. So you'd live in. She said the pay was not all that good but since it was rent-free, that made all the difference."

The walk from the bus stop was a long one, hampered by Cee's new white high-heeled shoes. Without stockings, her feet were chafing. She carried a shopping bag brimming with the little she owned and hoped she looked respectable in this beautiful, quiet neighborhood. The address of Dr. and Mrs. Scott revealed a large two-story house rising above a church-neat lawn. A sign with a name, part of which she couldn't pronounce, identified her future employer. Cee wasn't sure whether she should knock on the front door or look for one at the back. She chose the latter. A tall, stout woman opened the kitchen door. Reaching for Cee's shopping bag, she smiled. "You must be the one Reba called about. Step on in. My name is Sarah. Sarah Williams. The doctor's wife will see you shortly."

"Thank you, ma'am. Can I take off these shoes first?"

Sarah chuckled. "Whoever invented high heels won't be happy till they cripple us. Sit down. Let me give you a cold root beer."

Barefoot, Cee marveled at the kitchen — much, much bigger and better equipped than the one at Bobby's. Cleaner too. After a few swallows of root beer, she asked, "Can you tell me what-all I have to do?"

"Mrs. Scott will tell you some, but the doctor himself is the only one who really knows."

After a bathroom freshening, Cee put her shoes back on and followed Sarah into a living room that seemed to her more beautiful than a movie theater. Cool air, plum-colored velvet furniture, filtered light through heavy lace curtains. Mrs. Scott, her hands resting on a tiny pillow, her ankles crossed, nodded and, with a forefinger, invited Cee to sit.

"Cee, is it?" Her voice was like music.

"Yes, ma'am."

"Born here? Atlanta?"

"No, ma'am. I'm from a little place west of here, called Lotus."

"Any children?"

"No, ma'am."

"Married?"

"No, ma'am."

"What church affiliation? Any?"

"There's God's Congregation in Lotus but, I don't . . ."

"They jump around?"

"Ma'am?"

"Never mind. Did you graduate from high school?"

"No, ma'am."

"Can you read?"

"Yes, ma'am."

"Count?"

"Oh, yes. I even worked a cash register once."

"Honey, that's not what I asked you."

"I can count, ma'am."

"You may not need to. I don't really understand my husband's work — or care to. He is more than a doctor; he is a scientist and conducts very important experiments. His inventions help people. He's no Dr. Frankenstein."

"Dr. who?"

"Never mind. Just do what he says the way he wants and you'll be fine. Now go. Sarah will show you to your room."

Mrs. Scott stood up. Her dress was a kind of gown — floor-length white silk with wide sleeves. To Cee she looked every bit the queen of something who belonged in the movies.

Back in the kitchen, Cee saw that her shopping bag had been removed and Sarah was urging her to have something to eat before settling in. She opened the refrigerator and selected a bowl of potato salad and two fried chicken thighs.

"You want me to warm up this chicken?"

"No, ma'am. I like it just so."

"I know I'm old, but please call me Sarah."

"All right, if you want me to." Cee was surprised by her hunger. Being a habitual light eater, and surrounded by hot red meat sizzling in Bobby's kitchen, she was normally indifferent to food. Now she wondered if two pieces of chicken could even begin to dampen her appetite.

"How did it go, your meeting with Mrs. Scott?" asked Sarah.

"Fine," said Cee. "She's nice. Real nice."

"Uh-huh. She's easy to work for too. Has a schedule, certain likes and needs — never changes. Dr. Beau — that's what everybody calls him — is very gentlemanly."

"Dr. Beau?"

"His full name is Beauregard Scott."

Oh, thought Cee, that's how to say the name on the lawn sign. "They have any children?"

"Two girls. They're away. She tell you anything about what your work here is?"

"No. She said the doctor would do that. He's a scientist as well as a doctor, she said."

"It's true. She has all the money but he invents things. Tries to get patents for a lot of them."

"Patterns?" Cee's mouth was full of potato salad. "Like dress patterns?"

"No, girl. Like licenses to make things. From the government."

"Oh. Is there any more chicken, please? It's real good."

"Sure is, honey." Sarah smiled. "I'll fatten you up in no time if you stay here long enough."

"Was there other seconds working here? Did they get let go?" Cee looked anxious.

"Well, some quit. I remember just one who was fired."

"What for?"

"I never did find out what the matter was. He seemed just fine to me. Young he was and friendlier than most. I know they argued about something and Dr. Beau said he wouldn't have fellow travelers in his house."

"What's a fallow traveler?"

"Fellow, not fallow. Beats me. Something fierce, I reckon. Dr. Beau is a heavyweight Confederate. His grandfather was a certified hero who was killed in some famous battle up North. Here's a napkin."

"Thanks." Cee wiped her fingers. "Oh, I feel so much better now. Say, how long have you been working here?"

"Since I was fifteen. Let me show you to your room. It's downstairs and not much, but for sleep it's as good as anything. It's got a mattress made for a queen."

Downstairs was just a few feet below the front porch — more of a shallow extension of the house rather than a proper basement. Down a hall not far from the doctor's office was Cee's room, spotless, narrow, and without windows. Beyond it was a locked door leading to what Sarah said was a bomb shelter, fully stocked. She had placed Cee's shopping bag on the floor. Two nicely starched uniforms saluted from their hangers on the wall.

"Wait till tomorrow to put one on," said Sarah, adjusting the pristine collar of her handiwork.

"Oooh, this is nice. Look, a little desk." Cee gazed at the bed's headboard, then touched it with a grin. She shuffled her feet on the small rug lying next to the bed. Then, after peeping behind a folding screen to see the toilet and sink, she plopped on the bed, delighting in the thickness of the mattress. When she pulled the sheets back she giggled at its silk cover. So there, Lenore, she thought. What you sleep on in that broke-down bed you got? Remembering the thin, bumpy mattress Lenore slept on, she couldn't help herself and laughed with wild glee.

"Shh, girl. Glad you like it, but don't laugh so loud. It's frowned on here."

"Why is that?"

"Tell you later."

"No. Now, Sarah, please?"

"Well, remember those daughters I mentioned being away? They're in a home. They both have great big heads. Cephalitis, I think they call it. Sad for it to happen to even one, but two? Have mercy."

"Oh, my Lord. What a misery," said Cee, thinking, I guess that's why he invents things — he wants to help other folks.

The next morning, standing before her employer, Cee found him formal but welcoming. A small man with lots of silver hair, Dr. Beau sat stiffly behind a wide, neat desk. The first question he put to her was whether she had children or had been with a man. Cee told him she had been married for a spell, but had not gotten pregnant. He seemed pleased to hear that. Her duties, he said, were primarily cleaning instruments and equipment, tidying and keeping a schedule of patients' names, time of appointments and so on. He did his own billing in his office, which was separate from the examination/laboratory room.

"Be here promptly at ten in the morning," he said, "and be prepared to work late if the situation calls for it. Also, be prepared for the reality of medicine: sometimes blood, sometimes pain. You will have to be steady and calm. Always. If you can you'll do just fine. Can you do that?"

"Yes, sir. I can. I sure can."

And she did. Her admiration for the doctor grew even more when she noticed how many more poor people — women and girls, especially — he helped. Far more than the well-to-do ones from the neighborhood or from Atlanta proper. He was extremely careful with his patients, finicky about observing their privacy, except when he invited another doctor to join him in working on a patient. When all of his dedicated help didn't help and a patient got much worse he sent her to a charity hospital in the city. When one or two died in spite of his care, he donated money for funeral expenses. Cee loved her work: the beautiful house, the kind doctor, and the wages — never skipped or short as they sometimes were at Bobby's. She saw nothing of Mrs. Scott. Sarah, who took care of all her needs, said the lady of the house never left it and had a tiny laudanum craving. The doctor's wife spent much of her time painting flowers in watercolor or watching television shows. *Milton Berle* and *The Honeymooners* were her favorites. She had flirted with *I Love Lucy*, but hated Ricky Ricardo too much to watch it.

One day, a couple of weeks into the job, Cee entered Dr. Beau's office a half hour before he arrived. She was always in awe of the crowded bookshelves. Now she examined the medical books closely, running her finger over some of the titles: *Out of the Night*. Must be a mystery, she thought. Then *The Passing of the Great Race*, and next to it, *Heredity, Race and Society*.

How small, how useless was her schooling, she thought, and promised herself she would find time to read about and understand "eugenics." This was a good, safe place, she knew, and Sarah had become her family, her friend, and her confidante. They shared every meal and sometimes the cooking. When it was too hot in the kitchen, they ate in the backyard under a canopy, smelling the last of the lilacs and watching tiny lizards flick across the walkway.

"Let's go inside," said Sarah, on a very hot afternoon that first week. "These flies too mean today. Besides, I got some honeydews need eating before they soften."

In the kitchen, Sarah removed three melons from a peck basket. She caressed one slowly, then another. "Males," she snorted.

Cee lifted the third one, then stroked its lime-yellow peel, tucking her forefinger into the tiny indentation at the stem break. "Female," she laughed. "This one's a female."

"Well, hallelujah." Sarah joined Cee's laughter with a low chuckle. "Always the sweetest."

"Always the juiciest," echoed Cee.

"Can't beat the girl for flavor."

"Can't beat her for sugar."

Sarah slid a long, sharp knife from a drawer and, with intense anticipation of the pleasure to come, cut the girl in two.

CHAPTER
FIVE

Women are eager to talk to me when they hear my last name. Money? They snigger and ask the same questions: Who named me that or if anybody did. If I made it up to make myself feel important or was I a gambler or thief or some other kind of crook they should watch out for? When I tell them my nickname, what folks back home call me, Smart Money, they scream with laughter and say: Ain't no such thing as dumb money, just dumb folks. Got any more? You must have mine. No end of easy talk after that and it's enough to keep a friendship going way after it's dried up just so they can make lame jokes: Hey, Smart Money, gimmee some. Money, come on over here. I got a deal you gonna love.

Truthfully, other than getting lucky back in Lotus and some street girls in Kentucky, I've had only two regular women. I liked the small breakable thing inside each one. Whatever their personality, smarts, or looks, something soft lay inside each. Like a bird's breastbone, shaped and chosen to wish on. A little V, thinner than bone and lightly hinged, that I could break with a forefinger if I wanted to, but never did. Want to, I mean. Knowing it was there, hiding from me, was enough.

It was the third woman who changed everything. In her company the little wishbone V took up residence in my own chest and made itself at home. It was her forefinger that kept me on edge. I met her at a cleaner's. Late fall, it was, but in that ocean-lapped city, who could tell? Sober as sunlight, I handed her my army issue and couldn't take my eyes away from hers. I must have looked the fool, but I didn't feel like one. I felt like I'd come home. Finally. I'd been wandering. Not totally homeless, but close. Drinking and hanging out in music bars on Jackson Street, sleeping on the sofas of drinking buddies or outdoors, betting my forty-three dollars of army pay in crap games and pool halls. And when that was gone, I took quick day jobs until the next check came. I knew I needed help but there wasn't any. With no army orders to follow or complain about I ended up in the streets with none.

I remember exactly why I hadn't had a drink in four days and needed to dry-clean my clothes. It was because of that morning when I walked over by the bridge. A crowd was milling there along with an ambulance. When I got close enough I saw a medic's arms holding a little girl vomiting water. Blood ran from her nose. A sadness hit me like a pile-driver. My stomach fell and just the thought of whiskey made me want to heave. I rushed off feeling shaky, then I spent a few nights on benches in the park until the cops ran me off. When on the fourth day I caught my reflection in a store window I thought it was somebody else. Some dirty, pitiful-looking guy. He looked like the me in a dream I kept having where I'm on a battlefield alone. Nobody anywhere. Silence everywhere. I keep walking but I don't find anybody at all. Right then I decided to clean up. To hell with the dreams. I needed to make my homeboys proud. Be something other than a haunted, half-crazy drunk. So when I saw this woman at the cleaner's, I was wide open for her. If it wasn't for that letter, I'd still be hanging from her apron strings. She

56

had no competition in my mind except for the horses, a man's foot, and Ycidra trembling under my arm.

You are dead wrong if you think I was just scouting for a home with a bowl of sex in it. I wasn't. Something about her floored me, made me want to be good enough for her. Is that too hard for you to understand? Earlier you wrote about how sure I was that the beat-up man on the train to Chicago would turn around when they got home and whip the wife who tried to help him. Not true. I didn't think any such thing. What I thought was that he was proud of her but didn't want to show how proud he was to the other men on the train. I don't think you know much about love.

Or me.

CHAPTER
SIX

The actors were much nicer than the actresses. At least they called her by her name and didn't mind if their costume didn't quite fit or was stained from old makeup. The women called her "girl," as in "Where's the girl?" "Say, girl, where's my jar of Pond's?" And they raged when their hair or wigs didn't obey.

Lily's resentment was mild because seamstress/wardrobe was a financial promotion from cleaning woman and she got to show off the sewing skills her mother had taught her: slip stitch, blanket stitch, chain, back, yo-yo, shank-button, and flat. In addition, Ray Stone, the director, was polite to her. He produced two sometimes three plays a season at the Skylight Studio and taught acting classes the rest of the time. So, small and poor as it was, the theater was as busy as a hive all year. In between productions and after classes, the place hummed with intense argument, and sweat misted the foreheads of Mr. Stone and his students. Lily thought they were more animated then than when they were onstage. She couldn't help overhearing these quarrels, but she didn't understand anger that wasn't about a scene or how to say some lines. Now that the Skylight was shut down, Mr. Stone arrested and she out of a job, it was clear she should have listened closely.

It must have been the play. The one that caused the problem, the picketing, then the visit from two government men in snap-brim hats. The play, from her point of view, wasn't very good. Lots of talking, very little action, but not so bad it had to be closed. Certainly not as bad as the one they rehearsed but couldn't get permission to perform. *The Morrison Case*, it was called, by somebody named Albert Maltz if her memory was right.

The pay was less at Wang's Heavenly Palace dry cleaners and there were no tips from actors. Yet working in daylight was an improvement over walking in darkness to get from her tiny rented room to the theater and back. Lily stood in the pressing room, recalling a recent irritation that had blossomed into anger. The response she had recently gotten from the real estate agent had her seething. Frugal and minding her own business, she had added enough to what her parents left her to leave the rooming house and put a down payment on a house of her own. She had circled an advertisement for a lovely one for five thousand dollars and, although it was far from her work at the cleaner's, she would happily commute from so nice a neighborhood. The stares she had gotten as she strolled the neighborhood didn't trouble her, since she knew how neatly dressed she was and how perfect her straightened hair. Finally, after a few afternoon strolls, she consulted a Realtor. When she described her purpose and the couple of houses on sale she had found, the agent smiled and said, "I'm really sorry."

"They're sold already?" asked Lily.

The agent dropped her eyes, then decided not to lie. "Well, no, but there are restrictions."

"On what?"

The agent sighed. Obviously not wanting to have this conversation, she lifted her desk blotter and pulled out some stapled papers. Turning a page, she showed Lily an underlined passage. Lily traced the lines of print with her forefinger:

No part of said property hereby conveyed shall ever be used or occupied by any Hebrew or by any person of the Ethiopian, Malay or Asiatic race excepting only employees in domestic service.

"I've got rentals and apartments in other parts of the city. Would you like . . ."

"Thank you," said Lily. She raised her chin and left the office as quickly as pride let her. Nevertheless, when her anger cooled and after some mulling, she returned to the agency and rented a second-floor one-bedroom apartment near Jackson Street.

Although her employers were far more considerate than the actresses at Skylight Studio, after six months of pressing and steaming for the Wangs, and even after they gave her a seventy-five-cent raise, she was feeling stifled. She still wanted to buy that house or one like it. Into that restlessness stepped a tall man with a bundle of army-issue clothes for "same-day" service. The Wang couple, at lunch in the back room, had left her to attend the counter. She told the customer the "same-day" service applied only if requests were made before noon; he could pick his things up the next day. She smiled when she spoke. He did not return the smile, but his eyes had such a quiet, faraway look — like people who made their living staring at ocean waves — she relented.

"Well, I'll see what I can do. Come back at five-thirty."

He did and, holding the clothes hangers over his shoulder, waited on the sidewalk for half an hour until she came out. Then he offered to walk her home.

"Do you want to come up?" Lily asked him.

"I'll do anything you say."

She laughed.

They slid into each other, becoming a couple of sorts within a week. But months later, when he said he had to leave her for family reasons, Lily felt one abnormal pulse beat. That was all.

Living with Frank had been glorious at first. Its breakdown was more of a stutter than a single eruption. She had begun to feel annoyance rather than alarm when she came home from work and saw him sitting on the sofa staring at the floor. One sock on, the other in his hand. Neither calling his name nor leaning toward his face moved him. So Lily learned to let him be and flounced off to the kitchen to clean up whatever mess he'd left. The times when it was as good as at the beginning, when she felt such sweetness waking up with him next to her, his dog tags under her cheek, had become memories she was less and less inclined to dredge up. She regretted the loss of ecstasy but assumed its heights would at some point return.

Meantime the small mechanics of life needed attention: unpaid bills, frequent gas leaks, mice, runs in her last pair of hose, hostile, quarreling neighbors, dripping faucets, frivolous heating, street dogs, and the insane price of hamburger. None of these irritations did Frank take seriously, and in all honesty she couldn't blame him. She knew that buried underneath the pile of complaints lay her yearning for her own house. It infuriated Lily that he shared none of her enthusiasm for achieving that goal. In fact he seemed to have no goals at all. When she questioned him about the future, what he wanted to do, he said, "Stay alive." Oh, she thought. The war still haunted him. So, whether annoyed or alarmed, she forgave him much: like that time in February when they went to a church convention held on a high school football field. Known more for table after table of delicious free food than for proselytizing, the church welcomed everybody. And everybody came — not only members of the congregation. The nonbelievers, crowding the entrance and lining up for food, outnumbered the believers. Literature passed out by serious-looking young people and sweet-faced elders was stuffed into purses and side pockets. When the morning rain stopped and sunlight sashayed through the clouds, Lily and Frank exchanged their slickers for sweaters and strolled hand in hand to the stadium. Lily held her chin a bit higher and wished Frank had had a haircut. People gave him more than a passing glance, probably because he was so tall, or so she hoped. Anyway, they were in high spirits all afternoon — chatting with people and helping children load their plates. Then, smack in the middle of all that cold sunlight and warm gaiety, Frank bolted. They had been standing at a table, piling seconds of fried chicken on their plates, when a little girl with slanty eyes reached up over the opposite edge of the table to grab a cupcake. Frank leaned over to push the platter closer to her. When she gave him a broad smile of thanks, he dropped his food and ran through the crowd. People, those he bumped into and others, parted before him — some with frowns, others simply agape. Alarmed and embarrassed, Lily put down her paper plate. Trying hard to pretend he was a stranger to her, she walked slowly, her chin up, making no eye contact, past the bleachers and away from the exit Frank had taken.

When she returned to the apartment, she was thankful to find it empty. How could he change so quickly? Laughing one second, terrified the next? Was there some violence in him that could be directed toward her? He had moods, of course, but was never argumentative or the least threatening. Lily drew up her knees and, with her elbows leaning on them, pondered her confusion and his, the future she wanted and the question of whether he could share it. Dawn light seeped through the curtains before he returned. Lily's heart jumped when she heard the key turn in the lock, but he was calm and, as he put it, "beat up with shame."

"Was it something to do with your time in Korea that spooked you?" Lily had never asked about the war and he had never brought it up. Good, she had thought. Better to move on.

Frank smiled. "My time?"

"Well, you know what I mean."

"Yeah, I know. It won't happen again. Promise." Frank enclosed her in his arms.

Things went back to normal. He worked at a car wash in the afternoons, she at Wang's weekdays and doing alterations on Saturdays. They did less and less socializing, but Lily didn't miss it. The occasional movie was enough until they sat through *He Ran All the Way*. Afterward Frank spent part of the night clenching his fist in silence. There were no more movies.

Lily's sights were set elsewhere. Little by little she was being singled out for her sewing skills. Twice she had made lace for a bridal veil and, after embroidering a linen tablecloth at the request of a well-to-do customer, her reputation grew. Receiving multiple special orders, she made up her mind to have her own place no matter what and open a dressmaking shop in it, perhaps becoming a costume designer someday. After all, she had professional experience in the theater.

As Frank promised, there was no other public explosion. Still. The multiple times when she came home to find him idle again, just sitting on the sofa staring at the rug, were unnerving. She tried; she really tried. But every bit of housework — however minor —

64

was hers: his clothes scattered on the floor, food-encrusted dishes in the sink, ketchup bottles left open, beard hair in the drain, waterlogged towels bunched on bathroom tiles. Lily could go on and on. And did. Complaints grew into one-sided arguments, since he wouldn't engage.

"Where were you?"

"Just out."

"Out where?"

"Down the street."

Bar? Barbershop? Pool hall. He certainly wasn't sitting in the park.

"Frank, could you rinse the milk bottles before you put them on the stoop?"

"Sorry. I'll do it now."

"Too late. I've done it already. You know, I can't do everything."

"Nobody can."

"But you can do something, can't you?"

"Lily, please. I'll do anything you want."

"What I want? This place is ours."

The fog of displeasure surrounding Lily thickened. Her resentment was justified by his clear indifference, along with his combination of need and irresponsibility. Their bed work, once so downright good to a young woman who had known no other, became a duty. On that snowy day when he asked to borrow all that money to take care of his sick sister in Georgia, Lily's disgust fought with relief and lost. She picked up the dog tags he'd left on the bathroom sink and hid them away in a drawer next to her bankbook. Now the apartment was all hers to clean properly, put things where they belonged, and wake up knowing they'd not been moved or smashed to pieces. The loneliness she felt before Frank walked her home from Wang's cleaners began to dissolve and in its place a shiver of freedom, of earned solitude, of choosing the wall she wanted to break through, minus the burden of shouldering a tilted man. Unobstructed and undistracted, she could get serious and develop a plan to match her ambition and succeed. That was what her parents had taught her and what she had promised them: To choose, they insisted, and not ever be moved. Let no insult or slight knock her off her ground. Or, as her father was fond of misquoting, "Gather up your loins, daughter. You named Lillian Florence Jones after my mother. A tougher lady never lived. Find your talent and drive it."

The afternoon Frank left, Lily moved to the front window, startled to see heavy snowflakes powdering the street. She decided to shop right away in case the weather became an impediment. Once outside, she spotted a leather change purse on the sidewalk. Opening it she saw it was full of coins — mostly quarters and fifty-cent pieces. Immediately she wondered if anybody was watching her. Did the curtains across the street shift a little? The passengers in the car rolling by — did they see? Lily closed the purse and placed it on the porch post. When she returned with a shopping bag full of emergency food and supplies the purse was still there, though covered in a fluff of snow. Lily didn't look around. Casually she scooped it up and dropped it into the groceries. Later, spread out on the side of the bed where Frank had slept, the coins, cold and bright, seemed a perfectly fair trade. In Frank Money's empty space real money glittered. Who could mistake a sign that clear? Not Lillian Florence Jones.

CHAPTER
SEVEN

Lotus, Georgia, is the worst place in the world, worse than any battlefield. At least on the field there is a goal, excitement, daring, and some chance of winning along with many chances of losing. Death is a sure thing but life is just as certain. Problem is you can't know in advance.

In Lotus you did know in advance since there was no future, just long stretches of killing time. There was no goal other than breathing, nothing to win and, save for somebody else's quiet death, nothing to survive or worth surviving for. If not for my two friends I would have suffocated by the time I was twelve. They, along with my little sister, kept the indifference of parents and the hatefulness of grandparents an afterthought. Nobody in Lotus knew anything or wanted to learn anything. It sure didn't look like anyplace you'd want to be. Maybe a hundred or so people living in some fifty spread-out rickety houses. Nothing to do but mindless work in fields you didn't own, couldn't own, and wouldn't own if you had any other choice. My family was content or maybe just hopeless living that way. I understand. Having been run out of one town, any other that offered safety and the peace of sleeping through the night and not waking up with a rifle in your face was more than enough. But it was much less than enough for me. You never lived there so you don't know what it was like. Any kid who had a mind would lose it. Was I supposed to be happy with a little quick sex without love every now and then? Maybe some accidental or planned mischief? Could marbles, fishing, baseball, and shooting rabbits be reasons to get out of bed in the morning? You know it wasn't.

Mike, Stuff, and me couldn't wait to get out and away, far away.

Thank the Lord for the army.

I don't miss anything about that place except the stars.

Only my sister in trouble could force me to even think about going in that direction.

Don't paint me as some enthusiastic hero.

I had to go but I dreaded it.

CHAPTER
EIGHT

Jackie's ironing was flawless. Her floor scrubbing was not as good, but Lenore kept her on because her skill with plackets, shirt cuffs, collars, and yokes could not be surpassed. It was a delight to see those small hands lift the heavy iron effortlessly, a pleasure to note how easily she manipulated the wood stove's flame. How adept she was at sensing how hot the metal, the difference between its scorch and its perfect temperature. She was twelve, with that combination of raucous child's play and adult execution of chores. You could see her in the road blowing bubblegum and handling a paddleball at the same time, or hanging upside down from an oak tree branch. Ten minutes later she might be scaling fish or plucking hens like a professional. Lenore blamed herself for the poor quality of Jackie's mopping. The head of the mop was made up of a bundle of rags, not the absorbent rope of better ones. She pondered telling her to scrub on her knees but chose not to observe that thin little girl body bent down on all fours. Salem had been asked repeatedly to get a new mop, to hitch a ride with Mr. Haywood to Jeffrey and buy the supplies they needed. His excuse: "You know how to drive. Go yourself," was one of many.

Lenore sighed and tried not to compare Salem with her first husband. My, my, what a sweet man, she thought. Not just caring, energetic and a good Christian, but a moneymaker too. He owned a gasoline station right where the main road split off into a country road, the ideal spot to need a tank refill. Sweet man. Awful, awful, that he was shot to death by someone who wanted or envied his gas station. The note left on his chest said "Get the hell out. Now." It happened during the deepest part of the Depression and the sheriff had more important things on his mind. Searching the county for a common shooting was not one of them. He took the note and said he'd look into it. If he did, he didn't say what he found. Fortunately, her husband had savings, insurance, and a piece of abandoned property belonging to his cousin in Lotus, Georgia. Frightened that whoever killed her husband might come after her, she sold the house, packed her car with all it could hold and moved from Heartsville, Alabama, to Lotus. Her fear dwindled over time, but not enough to be comfortable living alone. So marrying a Lotus widower named Salem Money solved that problem for a while anyway. Looking for someone to help her fix the house, Lenore spoke to the pastor at God's Congregation church. He gave her one or two names, but hinted that Salem Money would have the time and the skill. It was true, and since Salem was one of the few unmarried men around, it seemed natural that they would join forces. They drove all the way to Mount Haven, Lenore at the wheel, for a marriage license that the clerk refused to issue because they did not have birth certificates. Or so she said. The arbitrariness of that denial, however, did not stop them. They took vows at God's Congregation.

Just as Lenore began to feel safe and comfortable so far from Alabama, a passel of Salem's relatives — ragged and run out of their home — arrived: his son Luther, the wife, Ida, another son, Frank, a grandson, also Frank, and a howling newborn baby girl.

It was impossible. All she and Salem had done to fix up the house was for nothing. She had to plan ahead to use the outhouse; there was no privacy at all. Waking up early for a leisurely breakfast, as was her habit, she had to step over the sleeping or nursing or snoring bodies scattered through her house. She adjusted and had her breakfast when the men left and Ida took the baby to the fields with her. But it was the infant's night crying that infuriated her most. When Ida asked Lenore if she would care for the baby because she could no longer see to her in the field, Lenore thought she would lose her mind. She could hardly refuse, but agreed mainly because the four-year-old brother was clearly the real mother to the infant.

Those three years were a trial even though the homeless family was grateful, doing whatever she wished and never complaining. They were allowed to keep all of their wages because when they had saved enough they could rent their own place and leave hers. Tight quarters, inconvenience, extra chores, an increasingly indifferent husband — her haven was destroyed. The cloud of her displeasure at being so put-upon found a place to float: around the heads of

72

the boy and girl. It was they who paid, although Lenore believed she was merely a strict step-grandmother, not a cruel one.

The girl was hopeless and had to be corrected every minute. The circumstances of her birth did not bode well. There was probably a medical word for her awkwardness, for a memory so short even a switching could not help her remember to close the chicken coop at night, or not to spill food on her clothes every single day. "You got two dresses. Two! You expect me to wash one of them up after every meal?" Only the hatred in the eyes of her brother kept Lenore from slapping her. He was always protecting her, soothing her as though she were his pet kitten.

Finally the family moved into their own house. Peace and order reigned. Years passed, children grew and left, parents sickened and died, crops failed, storms knocked down homes and churches, but Lotus held on. Lenore also, until she began to feel dizzy too often. That's when she persuaded Jackie's mother to let the girl do certain chores for her. Her only hesitation was Jackie's dog, the girl's constant minder. A black and brown Doberman, it never left Jackie's side. Even when the girl was asleep or inside any house in the neighborhood, the Doberman lay its head between its paws right outside the door. Never mind, thought Lenore, as long as the dog remained in the yard or on her porch. She needed someone to do the chores that required sustained standing. Also from Jackie she could glean bits of news about what was going on in the village.

She learned that the city boy Cee had run off with had stolen Lenore's car and left her in less than a month. That she was too ashamed to come back home. Figures, thought Lenore. Everything she ever surmised about that girl was true. Even getting married legitimately was beyond her. Lenore had had to insist on some formality, some record, otherwise the couple would have just another lax "living together" arrangement. Having no obligations, left one of them free to steal a Ford and the other to deny responsibility.

Jackie also described the condition of two families that had lost sons in Korea. One was the Durhams, Michael's folks. Lenore remembered him as a nasty piece of work and close friends with Frank. And another boy named Abraham, son of Maylene and Howard Stone, the one they called "Stuff," was also killed. Frank alone of the trio survived. He, so the chatter went, was never coming back to Lotus. The reaction of the Durhams and the Stones to the deaths of their sons was appropriate, but you would have thought they were waiting for the bodies of saints to be sent home. Didn't they know or remember how all three of those boys angled for invitations to that hairdresser's house? Talk about loose. Talk about disgrace. Mrs. K., they called her. Uppity didn't do her justice. When Reverend Alsop went to see her and cautioned her not to entertain local teenagers, she threw a cup of hot coffee on his shirt. A few grandmothers had encouraged the Reverend to speak to her, but the fathers didn't care about Mrs. K.'s services, nor did the mothers. Teenagers had to learn somewhere and a local widow who didn't want their husbands was more of a boon than a sin. Besides, their own daughters were safer that way. Mrs. K. did not solicit or charge. Apparently she occasionally satisfied herself (and teenage boys) when her appetite sharpened. Besides, nobody styled hair better. Lenore would not go across the road to say "Good morning," let alone sit in the abomination of her kitchen.

All this she told Jackie, and although the girl's eyes glazed over, she didn't argue or contradict Lenore as Salem consistently did.

She was a profoundly unhappy woman. And, although she had married to avoid being by herself, disdain of others kept her solitary if not completely alone. What soothed her was a fairly fat savings account, owning property, and having one, actually two, of the few automobiles in the neighborhood. Jackie was as much company as she wanted. Besides a good listener and great worker, the girl was worth much more than the quarter Lenore paid her each day.

And then it stopped.

Mr. Haywood said somebody had thrown two puppies out of the bed of a truck right before his eyes. He braked, picked up the one that had not had its neck broken, a female, and brought her to Lotus for the children he gave comic books and candy to. Although a few were delighted and took care of the puppy, others teased it. Jackie, however, adored the dog, feeding and protecting her and teaching her tricks. No wonder she immediately latched on to Jackie, who loved her most. She named the dog Bobby.

Bobby didn't normally eat chickens. She preferred pigeons; their bones were sweeter. And she didn't hunt for food; she merely ate whatever meal was given her or that she came across. So the pullet that pecked for worms around Lenore's porch steps was a clear invitation. The stick that Lenore used to beat Bobby off the pullet's carcass was the same one she used to keep herself upright.

Jackie heard the yelps and let the iron burn its shape on a pillowcase in order to dash out of the house and rescue Bobby. Neither one returned to Lenore's house.

Without help or a supportive husband, Lenore was as alone as she had been after her first husband died, as she had been before marrying Salem. It was too late to curry friendship with neighboring women, who she had made sure knew their level and hers. Pleading with Jackie's mother was humiliating as well as fruitless since the answer was "Sorry." Now she had to be content with the company of the person she prized most of all — herself. Perhaps it was that partnership between Lenore and Lenore that caused the minor stroke she suffered on a sweltering night in July. Salem found her kneeling beside the bed and ran to Mr. Haywood's house. He drove her to the hospital in Mount Haven. There, after a long, perilous wait in the corridor, she finally received treatment that curtailed further damage. Her speech was slurred but she was ambulatory — if carefully so. Salem saw to her basic needs, but was relieved to learn he could not understand a word she spoke. Or so he said.

It was a testimony to the goodwill of churchgoing and God-fearing neighboring women that they brought her plates of food, swept the floors, washed her linen, and would have bathed her too, except her pride and their sensitivity forbade it. They knew that the woman they were helping despised them all, so they didn't even have to say out loud what they understood to be true: that the Lord Works in Mysterious Ways His Wonders to Perform.

CHAPTER
NINE

Korea.

You can't imagine it because you weren't there. You can't describe the bleak landscape because you never saw it. First let me tell you about cold. I mean cold. More than freezing, Korea cold hurts, clings like a kind of glue you can't peel off.

Battle is scary, yeah, but it's alive. Orders, gut-quickening, covering buddies, killing — clear, no deep thinking needed. Waiting is the hard part. Hours and hours pass while you are doing whatever you can to cut through the cold, flat days. Worst of all is solitary guard duty. How many times can you take off your gloves to see if your fingernails are going black or check your Browning? Your eyes and ears are trained to see or hear movement. Is that sound the Mongolians? They are way worse than the North Koreans. The Mongols never quit; never stop. When you think they are dead they turn over and shoot you in the groin. Even if you're wrong and they're as dead as a dopehead's eyes it's worth the waste of ammo to make sure.

There I was, hour after hour, leaning on a makeshift wall. Nothing to see but a quiet village far below, its thatched roofs mimicking the naked hills beyond, a tight cluster of frozen bamboo sticking up through snow at my left. That's where we dumped our garbage. I stayed alert as best I could, listening, watching for any sign of sloe eyes or padded hats. Most of the time nothing moved. But one afternoon I heard a thin crackling in the bamboo stands. A single something was moving. I knew it wasn't the enemy — they never came in ones — so I figured it was a tiger. Word was they roamed up in the hills, but nobody had seen one. Then I saw the bamboo part, low to the ground. A dog, maybe? No. It was a child's hand sticking out and patting the ground. I remember smiling. Reminded me of Cee and me trying to steal peaches off the ground under Miss Robinson's tree, sneaking, crawling, being as quiet as we could so she wouldn't see us and grab a belt. I didn't even try to run the girl off that first time, so she came back almost every day, pushing through bamboo to scavenge our trash. I saw her face only once. Mostly I just watched her hand moving between the stalks to paw garbage. Each time she came it was as welcome as watching a bird feed her young or a hen scratching, scratching dirt for the worm she knew for sure was buried there.

Sometimes her hand was successful right away, and snatched a piece of garbage in a blink. Other times the fingers just stretched, patting, searching for something, anything, to eat. Like a tiny starfish — left-handed, like me. I've watched raccoons more choosy raiding trash cans. She wasn't picky. Anything not metal, glass, or paper was food to her. She relied not on her eyes but on her fingertips alone to find nourishment. K-ration refuse, scraps from packages sent with love from Mom full of crumbling brownies, cookies, fruit. An orange, soft now and blackened with rot, lies just beyond her fingers. She fumbles for it. My relief guard comes over, sees her hand and shakes his head smiling. As he approaches her she raises up and in what looks like a hurried, even automatic, gesture she says something in Korean. Sounds like "Yum-yum."

She smiles, reaches for the soldier's crotch, touches it. It surprises him. Yum-yum? As soon as I look away from her hand to her face, see the two missing teeth, the fall of black hair above eager eyes, he blows her away. Only the hand remains in the trash, clutching its treasure, a spotted, rotting orange.

Every civilian I ever met in that country would (and did) die to defend their children. Parents threw themselves in front of their kids without a pause. Still, I knew there were a few corrupt ones who were not content with the usual girls for sale and took to marketing children.

Thinking back on it now, I think the guard felt more than disgust. I think he felt tempted and that is what he had to kill.

Yum-yum.

CHAPTER
TEN

The Georgian boasted a country-ham-and-red-gravy breakfast. Frank got to the station early to reserve a coach seat. He gave the ticket lady a twenty-dollar bill and she gave him three pennies' change. At three-thirty in the afternoon he boarded and settled into the reclining seat. In the half hour until the train pulled out of the station, Frank released the haunting images always ready to dance before his eyes.

Mike in his arms again thrashing, jerking, while Frank yelled at him. "Stay here, man. Come on. Stay with me." Then whispering, "Please, please." When Mike opened his mouth to speak, Frank leaned in close and heard his friend say, "Smart, Smart. Don't tell Mama." Later, when Stuff asked what he said, Frank lied. "He said, 'Kill the fuckers.'" By the time medics got there, the urine on Mike's pants had frozen and Frank had had to beat away pairs of black birds, aggressive as bombers, from his friend's body. It changed him. What died in his arms gave a grotesque life to his childhood. They were Lotus boys who had known each other before they were toilet-trained, fled Texas the same way, disbelieving the unbelievable malignance of strangers. As children they had chased after straying cows, made themselves a ballpark in the woods, shared Lucky Strikes, fumbled and giggled their way into sex. As teens they made use of Mrs. K., the hairdresser, who, depending on her mood, helped them hone their sexual skills. They argued, fought, laughed, mocked, and loved one another without ever having to say so.

Frank had not been brave before. He had simply done what he was told and what was necessary. He even felt nervous after a kill. Now he was reckless, lunatic, firing, dodging the scattered parts of men. The begging, the howling for help he could not hear clearly until an F-51 dropped its load on the enemies' nest. In the post-blast silence the pleas wafted like the sound of a cheap cello coming from a chute of cattle smelling their blood-soaked future. Now, with Mike gone, he was brave, whatever that meant. There were not enough dead gooks or Chinks in the world to satisfy him. The copper smell of blood no longer sickened him; it gave him appetite. Weeks later, after Red was pulverized, blood seeped from Stuff's blasted arm. Frank helped Stuff locate the arm twenty feet away half buried in the snow. Those two, Stuff and Red, were especially close. "Neck" was dropped from Red's nickname because, hating northerners more than them, he preferred to associate with the three Georgia boys — Stuff most of all. Now they were meat.

Frank had waited, oblivious of receding gunfire, until the medics left and the grave unit arrived. There was too little left of Red to warrant the space of a whole stretcher, so he shared his remains with another's. Stuff had gotten a whole stretcher to himself, though, and holding his severed arm in the connected one he lay on the stretcher and died on it before the agony got to his brain.

Afterward, for months on end, Frank kept thinking, "But I know them. I know them and they know me." If he heard a joke Mike would love, he would turn his head to tell it to him — then a nanosecond of embarrassment before realizing he wasn't there. And never again would he hear that loud laugh, or watch him entertain whole barracks with raunchy jokes and imitations of movie stars. Sometimes, long after he'd been discharged, he would see Stuff's profile in a car stopped in traffic until the heart jump of sorrow announced his mistake. Abrupt, unregulated memories put a watery shine in his eyes. For months only alcohol dispersed his best friends, the hovering dead he could no longer hear, talk to, or laugh with.

But before that, before the deaths of his homeys, he had witnessed the other one. The scavenging child clutching an orange, smiling, then saying, "Yum-yum," before the guard blew her head off

Sitting on the train to Atlanta, Frank suddenly realized that those memories, powerful as they were, did not crush him anymore or throw him into paralyzing despair. He could recall every detail, every sorrow, without needing alcohol to steady him. Was this the fruit of sobriety?

Just after dawn outside Chattanooga the train slowed, then stopped, for no apparent reason. It soon became clear that something needed repair and it might take an hour, maybe more. A few coach passengers moaned, others took advantage and against the instructions of the conductor stepped outside to stretch their legs. Sleeping-car passengers woke and called for coffee. Those in club cars ordered food and more drinks. The part of the track where the train had halted ran alongside a peanut farm, but one could see a feed-store sign two or three hundred yards beyond. Frank, restless but not irritable, strolled toward the feed store. It was closed at that hour, but next to it a small shop was open to sell soda pop, Wonder bread, tobacco, and other products local folk craved. Bing Crosby's "Don't Fence Me In" crackled through a radio's weak reception. The woman behind the counter was in a wheelchair but, quick as a hummingbird, glided to the freezer and extracted the can of Dr Pepper Frank asked for. He paid, winked at her, got a glare in return, then went outside to drink. The young sun was blazing and there was little standing to cast a shadow or provide shade, only the feed store, the shop, and one shambling broke-down house across the road. A brand-new Cadillac, gilded in sunlight, was parked in front. Frank crossed the road to admire the car. Its taillights were slivers like shark fins. Its windshield stretched wide above the hood. As he got closer he heard voices — women's voices — cursing and grunting behind the house. He walked down the side toward the squeals, expecting to see some male aggressor showing off. But there on the ground were two women fighting. Rolling around, punching, kicking the air, they beat each other in the dirt. Their hair and clothes were in disarray. The

84

surprise to Frank was a man standing near them, picking his teeth and watching. He turned when Frank approached. He was a big man with flat, bored eyes.

"What the fuck you lookin' at?" He didn't remove the toothpick.

Frank froze. The big man came right up to him and shoved his chest. Twice. Frank dropped his Dr Pepper and swung hard at the man, who, lacking agility like so many really big men, fell immediately. Frank leaped on the prone body and began to punch his face, eager to ram that toothpick into his throat. The thrill that came with each blow was wonderfully familiar. Unable to stop and unwilling to, Frank kept going even though the big man was unconscious. The women stopped clawing each other and pulled at Frank's collar.

"Stop!" they screamed. "You're killing him! You motherfucker, get off him!"

Frank paused and turned to look at the big man's rescuers. One bent down to cradle the man's head. The other wiped blood from her nose and called the big man's name. "Sonny. Sonny. Oh, honey." Then she dropped to her knees and tried to revive her pimp. Her blouse was torn down the back. It was a bright yellow.

Frank stood and, massaging his knuckles, moved quickly, half running, half loping back to the train. He was either ignored or not seen by the repair crew. Inside the door to the coach section a porter eyed his bloodstained hands and dusty clothes but said nothing. Fortunately, the toilet was near the entrance so Frank could catch his breath and clean up before walking down the aisle. Once seated, Frank wondered at the excitement, the wild joy the fight had given him. It was unlike the rage that had accompanied killing in Korea. Those sprees were fierce but mindless, anonymous. This violence was personal in its delight. Good, he thought. He might need that thrill to claim his sister.

CHAPTER
ELEVEN

Her eyes. Flat, waiting, always waiting. Not patient, not hopeless, but suspended. Cee. Ycidra. My sister. Now my only family. When you write this down, know this: she was a shadow for most of my life, a presence marking its own absence, or maybe mine. Who am I without her — that underfed girl with the sad, waiting eyes? How she trembled when we hid from the shovels. I covered her face, her eyes, hoping she hadn't seen the foot poking out of the grave.

The letter said "She be dead," I dragged Mike to shelter and fought off the birds but he died anyway. I held on to him, talked to him for an hour but he died anyway. I stanched the blood finally oozing from the place Stuff's arm should have been. I found it some twenty feet away and gave it to him in case they could sew it back on. He died anyway. No more people I didn't save. No more watching people close to me die. No more.

And not my sister. No way.

She was the first person I ever took responsibility for. Down deep inside her lived my secret picture of myself — a strong good me tied to the memory of those horses and the burial of a stranger. Guarding her, finding a way through tall grass and out of that place, not being afraid of anything —

snakes or wild old men. I wonder if succeeding at that was the buried seed of all the rest. In my little-boy heart I felt heroic and I knew that if they found us or touched her I would kill.

CHAPTER
TWELVE

Frank walked down Auburn Street across from the station on Walnut. A hairdresser, a short-order cook, a woman called Thelma — finally he got the make of car and the name of an unlicensed cabdriver who might take him to Cee's suburban workplace. Arriving late because of the delay near Chattanooga, he spent the day up and down Auburn Street collecting information. Now it was too late. The cabdriver wouldn't be at his post until early the next morning. Frank decided to get something to eat, walk around awhile, then look for a place to sleep.

He ambled along till twilight and was on his way to the Royal Hotel when some young in-training gangsters jumped him.

He liked Atlanta. Unlike Chicago, the pace of everyday life was human here. Apparently there was time in this city. Time to roll a cigarette just so, time to examine vegetables with the eye of a diamond cutter. And time for old men to gather outside a storefront and do nothing but watch their dreams go by: the gorgeous cars of criminals and the hip-sway of women. Time, too, to instruct one another, pray for one another, and chastise children in the pews of a hundred churches. It was that amused affection that led him to drop his guard. He'd had lots of sad memories, but no ghosts or nightmares for two days, and he was desperate for black coffee in the mornings, not the wake-up jolt whiskey once gave him. So, the night before the gypsy cab would be available, he strolled down the streets, taking in the sights on his way to the hotel. Had he been alert instead of daydreaming, he would have recognized that reefer and gasoline smell, the rapid sneaker tread as well as the gang breath — the odor of scared children depending on group bravery. Not military but playground. At the mouth of an alley.

But he missed it all and two of the five sneaks grabbed his arms from behind. He used his foot to stomp one of theirs and in the space left by the boy's howling fall, Frank swung around and broke the jaw of the other one with his elbow. That was when one of the final three brought a pipe down on his head. Frank fell and in the blur of pain felt the body search followed by limping and running feet. He crawled toward the street and sat in darkness against a wall until his eyesight cleared.

"Need help?" The silhouette of a man framed by a streetlight stood before him.

"What? Oh."

"Here." The man held out his hand to help Frank up.

Patting his pockets while still wobbly, Frank cursed. "Damn." They'd stolen his wallet. Grimacing, he rubbed the back of his head.

"Want me to call the cops, or not?"

"Hell, no. I mean, no, but thanks."

"Well, take this." The man stuffed a couple of dollar bills in Frank's jacket pocket.

"Oh, thanks. But I don't need any . . ."

"Forget it, brother. Stay in the light."

Later, sitting in an all-night diner, Frank remembered the Samaritan's long ponytail catching the light of a streetlamp. He gave up hope of a good night's sleep at the hotel. His nerves were taut and pinging so he chose to stay as long as he could there, playing with cups of black coffee and a plate of eggs. It wasn't going well. If only he had a car, but Lily wouldn't hear of it. She had other plans. As he poked the eggs his thoughts turned to what Lily must be doing, thinking. She had seemed relieved at his departure. And, truth be told, so was he. He was now convinced his attachment to her was medicinal, like swallowing aspirin. Effectively, whether she knew it or not, Lily displaced his disorder, his rage and his shame. The displacements had convinced him the emotional wreckage no longer existed. In fact, it was biding its time.

Tired and uneasy, Frank left the diner and wandered aimlessly down the streets, pausing suddenly when he heard a trumpet screech. The sound came from down a short flight of steps ending at a half-open door. Appreciative voices underscored the trumpet's squeal, and if anything could match his mood it was that sound. Frank went inside. He preferred bebop to blues and happy-making love songs. After Hiroshima, the musicians understood as early as anyone that Truman's bomb changed everything and only scat and bebop could say how. Inside the room, small and thick with smoke, a dozen or so very intense people faced a trio: trumpet, piano, and drums. The piece went on and on and, except for a few nodding heads, no one moved. Smoke hovered; minutes ticked by. The pianist's face was slick with sweat, as was the trumpeter's. The drummer's, however, was dry. Clearly, there would be no musical end; the piece would stop only when a player was exhausted at last, when the trumpet player took the horn out of his mouth and the pianist tickled the keys before executing a final run. But when it happened, when the pianist and the trumpeter were through, the drummer was not. He kept on and on. After a while his fellow musicians turned to look at him and recognized what they must have seen before. The drummer had lost control. The rhythm was in charge. After long minutes, the pianist stood and the trumpet player put down his horn. Both lifted the drummer from his seat and took him away, his sticks moving to a beat both intricate and silent. The audience clapped their respect and their sympathy. Following the applause a woman in a bright blue dress and another piano player took the stage. She sang a few bars of "Skylark," then broke into a scat that cheered everybody up.

Frank left when the place emptied. It was 4:00 a.m., two hours until Mr. Gypsy Cab was due. His headache less active, he sat on the curb to wait. It never arrived.

No car, no cab, no friends, no information, no plan — finding transportation from city to suburb in these parts was rougher than confronting a battlefield. It was

7:30a.m. when he boarded a bus filled with silent dayworkers, housekeepers, maids, and grown lawn boys. Once beyond the business part of the city, they dropped off the bus one by one like reluctant divers into inviting blue water high above the pollution below. Down there they would search out the debris, the waste, resupply the reefs, and duck the predators swimming through lacy fronds. They would clean, cook, serve, mind, launder, weed, and mow.

Thoughts of violence alternating with those of caution rushed through Frank as he watched for the right street sign. He had no idea what he would do once he got to where Cee was. Maybe, as with the drummer, rhythm would take charge. Maybe he too would be escorted away, flailing helplessly, imprisoned in his own strivings. Suppose no one was home. He would have to break in. No. He couldn't let things get so out of control that it would endanger Cee. Suppose — but there was no point in supposing on unfamiliar ground. By the time he saw the correct street sign, it was too late to pull the cord. He calmed down while walking back several blocks before arriving at the M.D. sign on the lawn of Beauregard Scott's house. Near the steps bloomed a dogwood tree, its blossoms snow-white with purple centers. He considered whether to knock on the front door or the back. Caution suggested the back.

"Where is she?"

The woman who opened the kitchen door did not question him. "Downstairs," she said.

"You Sarah?"

"I am. Be as quiet as you can." She nodded toward the stairs that led to the doctor's office and Cee's room.

When Frank got to the bottom of the stairs he saw through an open door a small white-haired man sitting at a large desk. The man looked up.

"What? Who are you?" The doctor's eyes widened then narrowed at the insult of being invaded by a stranger. "Get out of here! Sarah! Sarah?"

Frank moved closer to the desk.

"There's nothing to steal here! Sarah!" The doctor reached for the telephone. "I'm calling the police. Now!" His forefinger was in the dial's zero when Frank knocked the telephone out of his hand.

Knowing completely now the nature of the threat, the doctor opened his desk drawer and pulled out a gun.

A .38, thought Frank. Clean and light. But the hand that held it shook.

The doctor raised the gun and pointed it at what in his fear ought to have been flaring nostrils, foaming lips, and the red-rimmed eyes of a savage. Instead he saw the quiet, even serene, face of a man not to be fooled with.

He pulled the trigger.

The click from the empty chamber was both tiny and thunderous. The doctor dropped the gun and ran around the desk, past the intruder and up the stairs. "Sarah!" he shouted. "Call the police, woman! Did you let him in here?"

Dr. Beau then ran down the hallway, to where another telephone sat on a small table. Standing next to it was Sarah, her hand pressed firmly on the cradle. There was no mistaking her purpose.

Meanwhile Frank walked into the room where his sister lay still and small in her white uniform. Asleep? He felt her pulse. Light or none? He leaned in to hear breath or no breath. She was cool to the touch, none of the early warmth of death. Frank knew death and this was not it — so far. Glancing quickly around the little room, he noticed a pair of white shoes, a bedpan and Cee's pocket-book. He rummaged in the purse and shoved the twenty dollars he found there into his pocket. Then he knelt by Cee's bed, slid his arms under her shoulders and knees, cradled her in his arms, and carried her up the stairs.

Sarah and the doctor stood locked in an undecipherable stare. As Frank passed around them with his motionless burden, Dr. Beau cast him a look of anger-shaded relief. No theft. No violence. No harm. Just the kidnapping of an employee he could easily replace, although, knowing his wife, he dared not replace Sarah — not yet anyway.

"Don't overplay your hand," he told her.

"No, sir," answered Sarah, but her hand remained pressed down on the telephone until the doctor descended the stairs to his office.

Once Frank had fumbled and eased his way through the front door and reached the sidewalk, he turned to glance back at the house and saw Sarah standing in the door, shadowed by the dogwood blossoms. She waved. Good-bye — to him and Cee or perhaps to her job.

Sarah stood for a moment watching the pair disappear down the walkway. "Thank the Lord," she whispered, thinking that one more day would have surely been too late. She blamed herself almost as much as she blamed Dr. Beau. She knew he gave shots, had his patients drink medicines he made up himself, and occasionally performed abortions on society ladies. None of that bothered or alarmed her. What she didn't know was when he got so interested in wombs in general, constructing instruments to see farther and farther into them. Improving the speculum. But when she noticed Cee's loss of weight, her fatigue, and how long her periods were lasting, she became frightened enough to write the only relative Cee had an address for. Days passed. Sarah didn't know if her scary note had been received and was steeling herself to tell the doctor he had to call an ambulance when the brother knocked on the kitchen door. Thank God. Exactly the way old folks said: not when you call Him; not when you want Him; only when you need Him and right on time. If the girl dies, she thought, it wouldn't be under her care in the doctor's house. It would be in her brother's arms.

Some dogwood blossoms, drooping in the heat, fell as Sarah shut the door.

Frank raised Cee to her feet, draped her right arm around his neck. Her head on his shoulder, her feet not even mimicking steps, she was feather-light. Frank got to the bus stop and waited for what seemed like an eternity. He passed the time counting the fruit trees in almost all the yards — pear, cherry, apple, and fig.

There were very few passengers on the bus back to town, and he was relieved to be relegated to the back, where bench seats allowed the two of them space and protected passengers from the sight of a man carrying, dragging, an obviously beat-up, drunken woman.

When they left the bus, it took a while to locate a gypsy cab parked away from the line of licensed taxis waiting, and more time to persuade the driver to accept the probable ruin of his backseat.

"She dead?"

"Drive."

"I am driving, brother, but I need to know if I'm going to jail or not."

"I said, drive."

"Where we going?"

"Lotus. Twenty miles down Fifty-four."

"That'll cost you."

"Don't worry 'bout it." But Frank was worried. Cee looked close to the edge of life. Mixed in with his fear was the deep satisfaction that the rescue brought, not only because it was successful but also how markedly nonviolent it had been. It could have been simply, "May I take my sister home?" But the doctor had felt threatened as soon as he walked in the door. Yet not having to beat up the enemy to get what he wanted was somehow superior — sort of, well, smart.

"She don't look too good to me," said the driver.

"Look where you going, man. The road ahead ain't in your mirror."

"I'm doing it, ain't I? Speed limit is fifty-five, you know. I don't want no trouble with cops."

"You don't shut your mouth, police will be the best thing happen to you." Frank's voice was stern but his ears were pricked for the cry of a siren.

"She bleedin' on my seat? You have to pay me extra if she mess up my backseat."

"Say another word, just one, and you won't get a fucking dime."

The driver turned on his radio. Lloyd Price, full of joy and happiness, sang out "Lawdy Miss Clawdy."

Cee, unconscious, occasionally moaning, her skin now hot to his touch, was dead weight, so Frank had trouble fumbling in his pockets for the fare. Barely had the taxi door shut when dust and pebbles kicked up behind the tires as the driver got as fast and as far away as he could from Lotus and its dangerous bed-bug-crazy country folk.

Cee's toes scooted the gravel as the tops of her feet were dragged down the narrow road to Miss Ethel Fordham's house. Frank picked his sister up again and, carrying her tightly in his arms, mounted the porch steps. A group of children stood in the road fronting the yard watching a girl bat a paddleball like a pro. They shifted their gaze to the man and his burden. A beautiful black dog lying next to the girl rose up and seemed more interested in the scene than the children. While they stared at the man and woman on Miss Ethel's porch, their mouths opened wide. One boy pointed at the blood staining the white uniform and sniggered. The girl hit him on the head with her paddle, saying, "Shut it!" She recognized the man as the one who long ago had made a collar for her puppy.

A peck basket of green beans lay by a chair. On a small table were a bowl and paring knife. Through the screen door Frank heard singing. "Nearer, my God, to Thee . . ."

"Miss Ethel? You in there?" Frank hollered. "It's me, Smart Money. Miss Ethel?"

The singing stopped and Ethel Fordham peered through the screen door, not at him, but at the slight form in his arms. She frowned. "Ycidra? Oh, girl."

Frank couldn't explain and didn't try to. He helped Miss Ethel get Cee on the bed, after which she told him to wait outside. She pulled up Cee's uniform and parted her legs.

"Have mercy," she whispered. "She's on fire." Then, to the lingering brother, "Go snap those beans, Smart Money. I got work to do."

CHAPTER
THIRTEEN

It was so bright, brighter than he remembered. The sun, having sucked away the blue from the sky, loitered there in a white heaven, menacing Lotus, torturing its landscape, but failing, failing, constantly failing to silence it: children still laughed, ran, shouted their games; women sang in their backyards while pinning wet sheets on clotheslines; occasionally a soprano was joined by a neighboring alto or a tenor just passing by. "Take me to the water. Take me to the water. Take me to the water. To be baptized." Frank had not been on this dirt road since 1949, nor had he stepped on the wooden planks covering the rain's washed-out places. There were no sidewalks, but every front yard and backyard sported flowers protecting vegetables from disease and predators — marigolds, nasturtiums, dahlias. Crimson, purple, pink, and China blue. Had these trees always been this deep, deep green? The sun did her best to burn away the blessed peace found under the wide old trees; did her best to ruin the pleasure of being among those who do not want to degrade or destroy you. Try as she might, she could not scorch the yellow butterflies away from scarlet rosebushes, nor choke the songs of birds. Her punishing heat did not interfere with Mr. Fuller and his nephew sitting in the bed of a truck — the boy on a mouth organ, the man on a six-string banjo. The nephew's bare feet swayed; the uncle's left boot tapped out the beat. Color, silence, and music enveloped him.

This feeling of safety and goodwill, he knew, was exaggerated, but savoring it was real. He convinced himself that somewhere nearby pork ribs sizzled on a yard grill and inside the house there was potato salad and coleslaw and early sweet peas too. A pound cake cooled on top of an icebox. And he was certain that on the bank of the stream they called Wretched, a woman in a man's straw hat fished. For shade and comfort she would be sitting under the sweet bay tree, the one with branches spread like arms.

When he reached the cotton fields beyond Lotus, he saw acres of pink blossoms spread under the malevolent sun. They would turn red and drop to the ground in a few days to let the young bolls through. The planter would need help for the laying by and Frank would be in line then, and again for the picking when it was time. Like all hard labor, picking cotton broke the body but freed the mind for dreams of vengeance, images of illegal pleasure — even ambitious schemes of escape. Cutting into these big thoughts were the little ones. Another kind of medicine for the baby? What to do about an uncle's foot swollen so large he can't put it in a shoe? Will the landlord be satisfied with half the rent this time?

While Frank waited for the hiring all he thought about was whether Cee was getting better or worse.

Her boss back in Atlanta had done something — what, he didn't know — to her body and she was fighting a fever that wouldn't go down. That the calamus root Miss Ethel depended on wasn't working, he did know. But that was all he knew because he was blocked from visiting the sickroom by every woman in the neighborhood. If it weren't for the girl Jackie he would have known nothing at all. From her he learned that they believed his maleness would worsen her condition. She told him the women took turns nursing Cee and each had a different recipe for her cure. What they all agreed upon was his absence from her bedside.

That explained why Miss Ethel didn't even want him on her porch.

"Go on off somewhere," she told him, "and stay gone till I call for you."

Frank thought the woman looked seriously scared. "Don't you let her die," he said. "You hear me?"

"Get out." She waved him away. "You not helping, Mr. Smart Money, not with that evil mind-set. Go 'way, I said."

So he busied himself cleaning and repairing his parents' house that had been empty since his father died. With the little that was left of his shoe money and the rest of Cee's wages he had just enough to re-rent it for a few months. He rummaged a hole next to the cookstove and found the matchbox. Cee's two baby teeth were so small next to his winning marbles: a bright blue one, an ebony one, and his favorite, a rainbow mix. The Bulova watch was still there. No stem, no hands — the way time functioned in Lotus, pure and subject to anybody's interpretation.

Soon as the blossoms began to fall, Frank headed down the rows of cotton to the shed that the farm manager called his office. He had hated this place once. The dust blizzards it created when fallow, the thrips wars and blinding heat. As a boy assigned to trash work while his parents were far away in the productive fields, his mouth had been dry with fury. He messed up as much as he could so they would fire him. They did. His father's scolding didn't matter because he and Cee were free to invent ways to occupy that timeless time when the world was fresh.

If she died because some arrogant, evil doctor sliced her up, war memories would pale beside what he would do to him. Even if it took the rest of his life, even if he spent the balance of it in prison. In spite of having defeated the enemy without bloodletting, imagining the death of his sister he joined the other pickers who planned sweet vengeance under the sun.

It was late June by the time Miss Ethel sent Jackie to tell him he could stop by, and July when Cee was well enough to move into their parents' home.

Cee was different. Two months surrounded by country women who loved mean had changed her. The women handled sickness as though it were an affront, an illegal, invading braggart who needed whipping. They didn't waste their time or the patient's with sympathy and they met the tears of the suffering with resigned contempt.

First the bleeding: "Spread your knees. This is going to hurt. Hush up. Hush, I said."

Next the infection: "Drink this. You puke, you got to drink more, so don't."

Then the repair: "Stop that. The burning is the healing. Be quiet."

Later, when the fever died and whatever it was they packed into her vagina was douched out, Cee described to them the little she knew about what had happened to her. None of them had asked. Once they knew she had been working for a doctor, the eye rolling and tooth sucking was enough to make clear their scorn. And nothing Cee remembered — how pleasant she felt upon awakening after Dr. Beau had stuck her with a needle to put her to sleep; how passionate he was about the value of the examinations; how she believed the blood and pain that followed was a menstrual problem — nothing made them change their minds about the medical industry.

"Men know a slop jar when they see one."

"You ain't a mule to be pulling some evil doctor's wagon."

"You a privy or a woman?"

"Who told you you was trash?"

"How was I supposed to know what he was up to?" Cee tried to defend herself.

"Misery don't call ahead. That's why you have to stay awake — otherwise it just walks on in your door."

"But —"

"But nothing. You good enough for Jesus. That's all you need to know."

As she healed, the women changed tactics and stopped their berating. Now they brought their embroidery and crocheting, and finally they used Ethel Fordham's house as their quilting center. Ignoring those who preferred new, soft blankets, they practiced what they had been taught by their mothers during the period that rich people called the Depression and they called life. Surrounded by their comings and goings, listening to their talk, their songs, following their instructions, Cee had nothing to do but pay them the attention she had never given them before. They were nothing like Lenore, who'd driven Salem hard, and now, suffering a minor stroke, did nothing at all. Although each of her nurses was markedly different from the others in looks, dress, manner of speech, food and medical preferences, their similarities were glaring. There was no excess in their gardens because they shared everything. There was no trash or garbage in their homes because they had a use for everything. They took responsibility for their lives and for whatever, whoever else needed them. The absence of common sense irritated but did not surprise them. Laziness was more than intolerable to them; it was inhuman. Whether you were in the field, the house, your own backyard, you had to be busy. Sleep was not for dreaming; it was for gathering strength for the coming day. Conversation was accompanied by tasks: ironing, peeling, shucking, sorting, sewing, mending, washing, or nursing. You couldn't learn age, but adulthood was there for all. Mourning was helpful but God was better and they did not want to meet their Maker and have to explain a wasteful life. They knew He would ask each of them one question: "What have you done?"

Cee remembered that one of Ethel Fordham's sons had been murdered up North in Detroit. Maylene Stone had one working eye, the other having been pierced at the sawmill by a wood chip. No doctor was available or summoned. Both Hanna Rayburn and Clover Reid, lame from polio, had joined their brothers and husbands hauling lumber to their storm-damaged church. Some evil, they believed, was incorrigible, so its demise was best left to the Lord. Other kinds could be mitigated. The point was to know the difference.

The final stage of Cee's healing had been, for her, the worst. She was to be sun-smacked, which meant spending at least one hour a day with her legs spread open to the blazing sun. Each woman agreed that that embrace would rid her of any remaining womb sickness. Cee, shocked and embarrassed, refused. Suppose someone, a child, a man, saw her all splayed out like that?

"Nobody going to be looking at you," they said. "And if they do? So what?"

"You think your twat is news?"

"Stop worrying your head," Ethel Fordham advised her. "I'll be out there with you. The important thing is to get a permanent cure. The kind beyond human power."

So Cee, bridling with embarrassment, lay propped on pillows at the edge of Ethel's tiny back porch soon as the sun's violent rays angled in that direction. Each time anger and humiliation curled her toes and stiffened her legs.

"Please, Miss Ethel. I can't do this no more."

"Oh, be quiet, girl." Ethel was losing patience. "So far as I can tell every other time you opened your legs you was tricked. You think sunlight going to betray you too?"

The fourth time she did relax, since an hour of lying rigid was so tiring. She forgot about whether anybody was peeping through the Bantam cornstalks in Ethel's garden or hiding behind the sycamores beyond it. Whether ten days of that surrender to the sun helped her female parts or not, she would never know. What followed the final sun-smacking hour, when she was allowed to sit modestly in a rocking chair, was the demanding love of Ethel Fordham, which soothed and strengthened her the most.

The woman pulled a chair next to Cee's on the porch. She placed on the table between them a plate of oven-hot biscuits and a jar of blackberry jam. It was the first non-medicinal food Cee was allowed to eat and the first taste of sugar. Eyes fixed on her garden, Ethel spoke quietly.

"I knew you before you could walk. You had those big, pretty eyes. They was full of sadness, though. I seen how you tagged along with your brother. When he left you ran off with that waste of the Lord's air and time. Now you back home. Mended finally, but you might just run off again. Don't tell me you going to let Lenore decide again who you are? If you thinking about it, let me tell you something first. Remember that story about the goose and the golden eggs? How the farmer took the eggs and how greed made him stupid enough to kill the goose? I always thought a dead goose could make at least one good meal. But gold? Shoot. That was always the only thing on Lenore's mind. She had it, loved it, and thought it put her above everybody else. Just like the farmer. Why didn't he plow his land, seed it, and grow something to eat?"

Cee laughed and spread jam on another biscuit.

"See what I mean? Look to yourself. You free. Nothing and nobody is obliged to save you but you. Seed your own land. You young and a woman and there's serious limitation in both, but you a person too. Don't let Lenore or some trifling boyfriend and certainly no devil doctor decide who you are. That's slavery. Somewhere inside you is that free person I'm talking about. Locate her and let her do some good in the world."

Cee put her finger in the blackberry jar. She licked it.

"I ain't going nowhere, Miss Ethel. This is where I belong."

Weeks later Cee stood at the stove pressing young cabbage leaves into a pot of simmering water seasoned with two ham hocks. When Frank got off work and opened the door, he noticed again how healthy she looked — glowing skin, back straight, not hunched in discomfort.

"Hey," he said. "Look at you."

"Bad?"

"No, you looking good. Feeling better?"

"I'll say. Much, much better. Hungry? This is just a no-count meal. Want me to catch a hen?"

"No. Whatever you cooking is fine."

"I know you used to like Mama's fry-pan bread. I'll make some."

"Want me to slice up these tomatoes?"

"Uh-huh."

"What's all that stuff on the sofa?" A pile of cloth scraps had been there for days.

"Pieces for quilting."

"You ever need a quilt down here in your whole life?"

"No."

"Then why you making one?"

"Visitors buy them."

"What visitors?"

"People over in Jeffrey, Mount Haven. Miss Johnson from Good Shepherd buys them from us and markets them to tourists down in Mount Haven. If mine turns out to be any good, Miss Ethel might show it to her."

"Nice."

"More than nice. We scheduled for electricity soon and running water. Both cost money. An electric fan alone is worth it."

"Then when I get paid you could get yourself a Philco refrigerator."

"What we need with a cold box? I know how to can and anything else I need I go outside and pick, gather, or kill it. Besides, who cooks up in here, me or you?"

Frank laughed. This Cee was not the girl who trembled at the slightest touch of the real and vicious world. Nor was she the not-even-fifteen-year-old who would run off with the first boy who asked her. And she was not the household help who believed whatever happened to her while drugged was a good idea, good because a white coat said so. Frank didn't know what took place during those weeks at Miss Ethel's house surrounded by those women with seen-it-all eyes. Their low expectation of the world was always on display. Their devotion to Jesus and one another centered them and placed them high above their lot in life. They delivered unto him a Cee who would never again need his hand over her eyes or his arms to stop her murmuring bones.

"Your womb can't never bear fruit."

Miss Ethel Fordham told her that. Without sorrow or alarm, she had passed along the news as though she'd examined a Burpee seedling overcome by marauding rabbits. Cee didn't know then what to feel about that news, no more than what she felt about Dr. Beau. Anger wasn't available to her — she had been so stupid, so eager to please. As usual she blamed being dumb on her lack of schooling, but that excuse fell apart the second she thought about the skilled women who had cared for her, healed her. Some of them had to have Bible verses read to them because they could not decipher print themselves, so they had sharpened the skills of the illiterate: perfect memory, photographic minds, keen senses of smell and hearing. And they knew how to repair what an educated bandit doctor had plundered. If not schooling, then what?

110

Branded early as an unlovable, barely tolerated "gutter child" by Lenore, the only one whose opinion mattered to her parents, exactly like what Miss Ethel said, she had agreed with the label and believed herself worthless. Ida never said, "You my child. I dote on you. You wasn't born in no gutter. You born into my arms. Come on over here and let me give you a hug." If not her mother, somebody somewhere should have said those words and meant them.

Frank alone valued her. While his devotion shielded her, it did not strengthen her. Should it have? Why was that his job and not her own? Cee didn't know any soft, silly women. Not Thelma, or Sarah, or Ida, and certainly not the women who had healed her. Even Mrs. K., who let the boys play nasty with her, did hair and slapped anybody who messed with her, in or outside her hairdressing kitchen.

So it was just herself. In this world with these people she wanted to be the person who would never again need rescue. Not from Lenore through the lies of the Rat, not from Dr. Beau through the courage of Sarah and her brother. Sun-smacked or not, she wanted to be the one who rescued her own self. Did she have a mind, or not? Wishing would not make it so, nor would blame, but thinking might. If she did not respect herself, why should anybody else?

Okay. She would never have children to care about and give her the status of motherhood.

Okay. She didn't have and probably would never have a mate. Why should that matter? Love? Please.

Protection? Yeah, sure. Golden eggs? Don't make me laugh.

Okay. She was penniless. But not for long. She would have to invent a way to earn a living.

What else?

After Miss Ethel gave her the bad news, the older woman went into the backyard and stirred coffee grounds and eggshells into the soil around her plants. Blank and unable to respond to Ethel's diagnosis, Cee watched her. A small bag of garlic cloves hung from her apron strings. For the aphids, she said. An aggressive gardener, Miss Ethel blocked or destroyed enemies and nurtured plants. Slugs curled and died under vinegar-seasoned water. Bold, confident raccoons cried and ran away when their tender feet touched crushed newspaper or chicken wire placed around plants. Cornstalks safe from skunks slept in peace under paper bags. Under her care pole beans curved, then straightened to advertise their readiness. Strawberry tendrils wandered, their royal-scarlet berries shining in morning rain. Honeybees gathered to salute *Illicium* and drink the juice. Her garden was not Eden; it was so much more than that. For her the whole predatory world threatened her garden, competing with its nourishment, its beauty, its benefits, and its demands. And she loved it.

What in this world did Cee love? She would have to think about that.

Meantime her brother was there with her, which was very comforting, but she didn't need him as she had before. He had literally saved her life, but she neither missed nor wanted his fingers at the nape of her neck telling her not to cry, that everything would be all right. Some things, perhaps, but not everything.

"I can't have children," Cee told him. "Never." She lowered the flame under the pot of cabbage.

"The doctor?"

"The doctor."

"I'm sorry, Cee. Really sorry." Frank moved toward her.

"Don't," she said, pushing his hand away. "I didn't feel anything at first when Miss Ethel told me, but now I think about it all the time. It's like there's a baby girl down here waiting to be born. She's somewhere close by in the air, in this house, and she picked me to be born to. And now she has to find some other mother." Cee began to sob.

"Come on, girl. Don't cry," whispered Frank.

"Why not? I can be miserable if I want to. You don't need to try and make it go away. It shouldn't go away. It's just as sad as it ought to be and I'm not going to hide from what's true just because it hurts." Cee wasn't sobbing anymore, but the tears were still running down her cheeks.

Frank sat down, clasped his hands and leaned his forehead on them.

"You know that toothless smile babies have?" she said. "I keep seeing it. I saw it in a green pepper once. Another time a cloud curved in such a way it looked like . . ." Cee didn't finish the list. She simply went to the sofa, sat and began sorting and re-sorting quilt

113

pieces. Every now and then she wiped her cheeks with the heel of her hand.

Frank stepped outside. Walking back and forth in the front yard, he felt a fluttering in his chest. Who would do that to a young girl? And a doctor? What the hell for? His eyes burned and he blinked rapidly to forestall what could have become the crying he had not done since he was a toddler. Not even with Mike in his arms or whispering to Stuff had his eyes burned that way. True, his vision was occasionally deceitful, but he had not cried. Not once.

Confused and deeply troubled, he decided to walk it off. He went down the road, cut through paths and skirted backyards. Waving occasionally at passing neighbors or those doing chores on their porches, he could not believe how much he had once hated this place. Now it seemed both fresh and ancient, safe and demanding. When he found himself on the bank of Wretched, the sometimes stream, sometimes creek, other times a bed of mud, he squatted beneath the sweet bay tree. His sister was gutted, infertile, but not beaten. She could know the truth, accept it, and keep on quilting. Frank tried to sort out what else was troubling him and what to do about it.

CHAPTER
FOURTEEN

I have to say something to you right now. I have to tell the whole truth. I lied to you and I lied to me. I hid it from you because I hid it from me. I felt so proud grieving over my dead friends. How I loved them. How much I cared about them, missed them. My mourning was so thick it completely covered my shame.

Then Cee told me about seeing a baby girl smile all through the house, in the air, the clouds. It hit me. Maybe that little girl wasn't waiting around to be born to her. Maybe it was already dead, waiting for me to step up and say how.

I shot the Korean girl in her face.

I am the one she touched.

I am the one who saw her smile.

I am the one she said "Yum-yum" to.

I am the one she aroused.

A child. A wee little girl.

I didn't think. I didn't have to.

Better she should die.

How could I let her live after she took me down to a place I didn't know was in me?

How could I like myself, even be myself if I surrendered to that place where I unzip my fly and let her taste me right then and there?

And again the next day and the next as long as she came scavenging.

What type of man is that?

And what type of man thinks he can ever in life pay the price of that orange?

You can keep on writing, but I think you ought to know what's true.

CHAPTER
FIFTEEN

The next morning at breakfast Cee appeared to have returned to her newly steady self, confident, cheerful and occupied. Spooning fried onions and potatoes into Frank's plate she inquired whether or not he wanted eggs too.

He declined, but asked for more coffee. He had spent a sleepless night, churning and entangled in thoughts relentless and troubling. How he had covered his guilt and shame with big-time mourning for his dead buddies. Day and night he had held on to that suffering because it let him off the hook, kept the Korean child hidden. Now the hook was deep inside his chest and nothing would dislodge it. The best he could hope for was time to work it loose. Meantime there were worthwhile things that needed doing.

"Cee?" Frank, glancing at her face, was pleased to see that her eyes were dry and calm. "What happened to that place we used to sneak off to? Remember? They had some horses over there."

"I remember," said Cee. "I heard some folks bought it for a place to play cards. Gambling night and day. And they had women in there too. After that I heard they ran dogfights."

"What did they do with the horses? Anybody know?"

"I don't. Ask Salem. He don't say nothing but he knows everything going on."

Frank had no intention of entering Lenore's house to locate Salem. He knew exactly when and where to find him. The old man was as regular in his habits as a crow. He perched on a friend's porch at a certain time, flew off to Jeffrey on a certain day, and trusted neighbors to feed him snacks between meals. As always, after supper he settled among the flock on Fish Eye Anderson's porch.

Except for Salem, the men there were veterans. The two oldest fought in the First World War, the rest battled in the Second. They knew about Korea but not understanding what it was about didn't give it the respect — the seriousness — Frank thought it deserved. The veterans ranked battles and wars according to loss numbers: three thousand at this place, sixty thousand in the trenches, twelve thousand at another. The more killed, the braver the warriors, not the stupider the commanders. Although he had no military stories or opinions, Salem Money was an avid player. Now that his wife was forced to spend most of her time in bed or in a lounge chair he was as close to freedom as he'd ever been. Of course he had to listen to her complaints, but her speech difficulty helped him pretend not to understand what she was on about. Another benefit was that he handled the money now. Each month he caught a ride to Jeffrey and took what was needed from their bank account. If Lenore asked to see the bankbook he ignored her or said, "Don't worry none. Every dime is fine."

After supper on almost any day Salem and his friends gathered to play checkers, chess, and once in a while whist. Two tables were permanent fixtures on Fish Eye's cluttered porch. Fishing poles leaned against the railing, vegetable baskets waited to be taken home, empty soda pop bottles, newspapers — all the gatherings that made men comfortable. While two pairs of players moved pieces around, the others leaned on the railing to chuckle, give advice, and tease the losers. Frank stepped over a basket of Detroit Dark Red beets and eased himself into the group of onlookers. As soon as the game of whist was over he moved to the chessboard, where Salem and Fish Eye pondered long minutes between moves. Into one of these pauses he spoke.

"Cee tells me that place yonder — with the horses — the one that used to be a stud farm. She says it runs dogfights now. That so?"

"Dogfights." Salem covered his mouth to funnel the laugh coming out.

"Why you laughing?"

"Dogfights. Pray that was all they done. No. That place burned down a while back, thank the sweet Lord." Salem waved his hand, urging Frank not to dislodge his concentration on his next move.

"You want to know about them dogfights?" asked Fish Eye. He seemed relieved by the interruption. "More like men-treated-like-dog fights."

Another man spoke up. "You didn't see that boy come through here crying? What did he call himself? Andrew, you 'member his name?"

"Jerome," said Andrew. "Same as my brother's. That's how come I remember."

"That's him. Jerome." Fish Eye slapped his knee. "He told us they brought him and his daddy from Alabama. Roped up. Made them fight each other. With knives."

"No sir. Switchblades. Yep, switchblades." Salem spat over the railing. "Said they had to fight each other to the death."

"What?" Frank felt his throat closing.

"That's right. One of them had to die or they both would. They took bets on which one." Salem frowned and squirmed in his chair.

"Boy said they slashed each other a bit — just enough to draw a line of blood. The game was set up so only the one left alive could leave. So one of them had to kill the other." Andrew shook his head.

The men became a chorus, inserting what they knew and felt between and over one another's observations.

"They graduated from dogfights. Turned men into dogs."

"Can you beat that? Pitting father against son?"

"Said he told his daddy, 'No, Pa. No.' "

"His daddy told him, 'You got to.' "

"That's a devil's decision-making. Any way you decide is a sure trip to his hell."

"Then, when he kept on saying no, his daddy told him, 'Obey me, son, this one last time. Do it.' Said he

120

told his daddy, 'I can't take your life.' And his daddy told him, 'This ain't life.' Meantime the crowd, drunk and all fired up, was going crazier and crazier, shouting, 'Stop yapping. Fight! God damn it! Fight!'"

"And?" Frank was breathing hard.

"And what you think? He did it." Fish Eye was furious all over again. "Come over here crying and told us all about it. Everything. Poor thing. Rose Ellen and Ethel Fordham collected some change for him so he could go on off somewhere. Maylene too. We all pulled together some clothes for him. He was soaked in blood."

"If the sheriff had seen him dripping in blood, he'd be in prison this very day."

"We led him out on a mule."

"All he won was his life, which I doubt was worth much to him after that."

"I don't believe they stopped that mess till Pearl Harbor," Salem said.

"When was this?" Frank clamped his jaw.

"When was what?"

"When the son, Jerome, came here."

"Long time. Ten or fifteen years, I reckon."

Frank was turning to leave when another question surfaced. "By the way, what happened to the horses?"

"I believe they sold 'em," said Salem.

Fish Eye nodded. "Yep. To a slaughterhouse."

"What?" That's hard to believe, thought Frank.

"Horse was the only meat not rationed during the war, see," said Fish Eye. "Ate some myself in Italy. France too. Tastes just like beef but sweeter."

121

"You ate some in the good old U.S.A. too, but you didn't know it." Andrew laughed.

Salem, impatient to get back to the chessboard, changed the subject. "Say, how's your sister?"

"Mended," Frank answered. "She'll be all right."

"She say what happened to my Ford?"

"That would be the last thing on her mind, Grandpappy. And it should be the last thing on yours."

"Yeah, well." Salem moved his queen.

CHAPTER
SIXTEEN

Cee refused to give up the quilt. Frank wanted it for something, something that was bothering him. The quilt was the first one she had made by herself. As soon as she could sit up without pain or bleeding, neighborhood women took over the sickroom and started sorting pieces while they discussed her medications and the most useful prayers Jesus would take notice of. They sang, too, while they stitched together the palette they had agreed upon. She knew her own quilt wasn't very good, but Frank said it was perfect. Perfect for what? He wouldn't say.

"Come on, Cee. I need it. And you have to come with me. Both of us have to be there."

"Be where?"

"Trust me."

He was late for dinner and when he came through the door he was perspiring and out of breath as though he had been running. A piece of sanded wood the size of a ruler stuck out of his back pocket. And he held a shovel.

Cee told him no. Absolutely not. Sloppy as the quilt was, she treasured its unimpressive pattern and haphazard palette. Frank insisted. By his perspiration and the steel in his eyes Cee understood that whatever he was up to was very important to him. Reluctantly she slid on her sandals and followed him, embarrassed again by the mediocrity of the quilt he carried over his shoulder. Perhaps anyone who saw them would think they were going out to fish. At five o'clock? With a shovel? Hardly.

They walked toward the edge of town, then turned onto a wagon road — the same one they had followed as children. When Cee, handicapped by her thin sandals, kept stumbling on the stones, Frank slowed his pace and took her hand in his. There was no point in questioning him. Just as long ago, when they ventured hand in hand into unknown territory, Cee accompanied her big brother silently. As annoyed as she was now at her relapse into doing what others wanted, she nevertheless cooperated. This one time, she told herself. I don't want Frank making decisions for me.

Perceptions alter: fields shrink as age increases; a half-hour wait is as long as a day for a child. The five rocky miles they traveled took the same two hours it had when they were children, yet then it seemed forever and far, far from home. The fencing that had been so sturdy had fallen down in most places — its duplicate threatening signs, some sporting the outline of a skull, were gone or mere shadow warnings poking through tall grass. As soon as Cee recognized the place, she said, "It's all burned down. I didn't know that, did you?"

"Salem told me, but we're not going there." Frank shielded his eyes for a moment before moving off, tracking what was left of the fencing. Suddenly he stopped and tested the earth, trampling through grass, tamping it in places, until he found what he was looking for.

"Yeah," he said. "Right here." He exchanged the quilt for the shovel and began digging.

Such small bones. So few pieces of clothing. The skull, however, was clean and smiling.

Cee bit her lip, forcing herself not to look away, not to be the terrified child who could not bear to look directly at the slaughter that went on in the world, however ungodly. This time she did not cringe or close her eyes.

Carefully, carefully, Frank placed the bones on Cee's quilt, doing his level best to arrange them the way they once were in life. The quilt became a shroud of lilac, crimson, yellow, and dark navy blue. Together they folded the fabric and knotted its ends. Frank handed Cee the shovel and carried the gentleman in his arms. Back down the wagon road they went, then turned away from the edge of Lotus toward the stream. Quickly they found the sweet bay tree — split down the middle, beheaded, undead — spreading its arms, one to the right, one to the left. There at its base Frank placed the bone-filled quilt that was first a shroud, now a coffin. Cee handed him the shovel. While he dug she watched the rippling stream and the foliage on its opposite bank.

"Who's that?" Cee pointed across the water.

"Where?" Frank turned to see. "I don't see anybody."

"He's gone now, I guess." But she was not sure. It looked to her like a small man in a funny suit swinging a watch chain. And grinning.

Frank dug a four- or five-foot hole some thirty-six inches wide. It took some maneuvering because the sweet bay roots resisted disturbance and fought back. The sun had reddened and was about to set. Mosquitoes trembled above the water. Honeybees had gone home. Fireflies waited for night. And a light smell of muscadine grapes pierced by hummingbirds soothed the gravedigger. When finally it was done a welcome breeze rose. Brother and sister slid the crayon-colored coffin into the perpendicular grave. Once it was heaped over with soil, Frank took two nails and the sanded piece of wood from his pocket. With a rock he pounded it into the tree trunk. One nail bent uselessly, but the other held well enough to expose the words he had painted on the wooden marker.

Here Stands A Man.

Wishful thinking, perhaps, but he could have sworn the sweet bay was pleased to agree. Its olive-green leaves went wild in the glow of a fat cherry-red sun.

CHAPTER
SEVENTEEN

I stood there a long while, staring at that tree.
It looked so strong
So beautiful.
Hurt right down the middle
But alive and well.
Cee touched my shoulder
Lightly.
Frank?
Yes?
Come on, brother. Let's go home.